Lonestar Loathsome
Tales of Murder, Monsters, and Mayhem
Nathan Klayman

ISBN: 979-8-218-46971-9

CONTENTS

I

HARMADILLOS

Fear, Fried Pies and Local Wildlife Up Close

They had just finished breakfast and were walking across the lot of Wanda's Lakeside – "Open 24/6! World-Famous Fried Pies!" – to where Ed's truck was parked when they first saw it. Or rather, Jim did. Ed had decided to wear his newest boots that day and had been keeping his eyes down to avoid Wanda's nearly world-famous parking lot potholes. He was so focused that he didn't see that Jim had stopped, causing a collision that almost sent him into a hole big enough to drown a healthy family of four.

Ed glared at Jim. "Goddamnit, Jim – cain't you watch where you're going? Ain't like these are new boots or nothin', or that the damn potholes here won't just about suck 'em off your feet. Damn, man." Scowling, he looked to make sure his boots were still on his feet and relatively unharmed.

Jim ignored this. He nudged Ed in the ribs. "Lookit that, Ed. Over there, near them dumpsters. See it?" He pointed.

Ed squinted, trying to follow Jim's finger while deciding if he should wait to say anything else mean. Then he saw what Jim was all excited about. "Oohhh." Over in the brush by the dumpsters was a smallish armadillo, rooting around unconcernedly for bugs. He snickered. "Man, I tell you, ain't much funnier than the way them dudes jump when scared. Like they wanna jump outta their shells!" Ed laughed some more.

Jim shrugged. "I always kinda liked 'em. Like lil prehistoric dinosaur dudes or something, I dunno." He went back to watching the armadillo.

Ed snorted. "Dinosaurs. Shit. You watch too much of that Animal Planet crap."

He looked over at the armadillo, a small smile twitching at the corner of his mouth. "Watch and learn." Ed turned away from the truck and began slowly creeping toward the dumpster.

Watching Ed with one eye, Jim kept looking at the armadillo, who still had given no indication that anything was approaching, let alone about to happen. It dug contentedly in the soil near the dumpster, occasionally twitching its ears. Jim was torn. He wanted to stop Ed from whatever it was he intended but didn't want to be the one to scare the creature either.

Ed was but a few feet away when the armadillo suddenly stopped rooting around. It sat back on its haunches, sniffing the air as though it suspected something. This caused Ed to freeze in his tracks, unmoving. The armadillo turned its head to and fro, scenting the air in search of possible danger. As it cast about, it looked over in Jim's direction. It lingered a second, staring, before deciding whatever danger there was had passed and lowered its head down.

Jim was unnerved. For a split second, it seemed like not only had the animal been looking directly at him, but its eye had...well, had glowed *red*, like it was lit up from inside. That's impossible, he thought. Armadillos don't have red eyes. They'd have mentioned that on that show if they did. Still, this bothered Jim, and he broke his silence, whispering, "Psst. Ed. Thinkin' maybe you don't wanna do this. C'mon back. Let's get."

Ed shook his head and made a motion that was part dismissive hand flap and part rude gesture. He crept forward towards the unsuspecting animal. Suddenly, he sprang forward, arms pistoning out, fingers hooked into claws, yelling in hopes of frightening the hapless creature, who obliged Ed by screaming as it leapt into the air. Returning to earth, it scuttled off into the brush as Ed wheezed with laughter.

Jim looked at him in disgust. "Well, that was mean. I sure hope it was worth it." He paused. "And don't look now, but you done fucked up them nice new boots." Jim picked up his pace and walked over to Ed's truck. "C'mon now. You had your laugh. Let's get out of here."

Ed picked himself up and looked at his boots. "Eh, just some mud. Totally worth it." He fished his keys out of his pocket. "Oh, don't get all upset now, Animal Planet. I didn't hurt that 'dillo none. Just scared him a bit." He slid behind the wheel as Jim stood there. "Well, come on then. Get in."

Jim sighed and got in the truck.

As they drove away, Jim turned towards Ed. "You notice anything funny about that 'dillo, Ed?" Ed snorted. "You mean, anything other than the way it screamed and jumped? Can't say that I did, but then hard to get much funnier than that." He laughed. Jim said nothing. Finally, Ed said, "I suppose you saw something, and you wanna tell me about it, maybe make me feel bad about scaring that critter, huh." He laughed again. "Want me to turn around, find that 'dillo, maybe buy it a fried pie to make up?"

At this, Jim just rolled his eyes. He started to speak, but as they crested the hill, he caught sight of something that made the words dry up in his throat. He threw a restraining arm up against Ed's chest, a strangled noise managing to escape. This made Ed slam on the brakes. "What the fuck, Jim?! We coulda been killed, you doin' that!" he screamed. Jim just pointed.

"Look," he whispered.

Ed looked. There, in the road, was an armadillo. It sat, unmoving, as if it had been waiting for them to come. Though shadowed by the tree that hung over this particular stretch of 208, they could see what looked like red eyes glowing at them. "You see that, Ed?"

Ed stared, as if unable to believe what he saw. Finally, he found his voice. "Think I see something that better know how to get outta the way of this truck, knows what's good for it." Truck still in park, Ed revved the engine.

The armadillo did not move.

Ed revved higher, making the engine scream and the tires smoke.

Still, the armadillo did not move.

Ed dropped the truck into Drive. "Fuck this shit," he ground out between his teeth. Raising his voice, he screamed, "IT WAS A GODDAMN JOKE!" and aimed the truck directly at the armadillo, who did not move.

Jim closed his eyes, not wanting to witness the slaughter – only to open them again in horror as the windshield shattered inward in a rain of glass. He heard Ed yell as he threw his hands up to shield his face from the worst of the glass, screaming for Ed as they careened wildly. If Ed responded, it was lost under the sounds of screeching and the scream of the truck engine. Jim felt something warm and wet hit the side of his face.

When the truck hit the old oak, the impact was hard enough to throw Jim from the cab through the now glassless front. In the seconds before he connected with the tree, hard enough to shatter most of his ribs and pulping several organs, he thought he saw what looked like the armadillo from the diner, eyes glowing red as it tore out Ed's eyes in a shower of gore.

"That can't be right," thought Jim. "Armadillos don't have red eyes. And they can't break glass. There's gotta be a mistake somewhere. I'm just imagining all this." Still unsure of what all had happened, Jim shivered, and closed his eyes.

The truck's engine ticked and cooled, along with both bodies. The sun moved along, and the sky darkened. As night fell, armadillos emerged, snuffling around the tree. They stepped over the corpses in an unhurried fashion, daintily avoiding the congealing pools as they searched for insects under leaves stippled with bits of brain and blood. Soon, there was only the sound of armadillos rooting, punctuated by the sound of cicadas in the distance.

2

A DROUGHT UNTO THE GENERATIONS

As a small child, I lived in a tiny town in the westernmost part of Texas. It was small enough to be forgotten about by better maps but had just enough of a toehold to warrant its own post office and grocery store.

We had running water and electricity, but according to local legend, no rain in over a hundred years. This may all seem like an exaggeration; certainly, it feels like it when setting it all down in black and white. But in all my time there, it never rained – not a single drop.

Weather talk was a popular conversation topic in our town, as it often is in many small towns where time is long like summer shadows and news scarce. I doubt that other towns were as focused on this subject as we were, but then why would they be? The clouds moved and changed where they were.

I grew up there in a small, unexpanded circle of parched, lazy tempers and jokes about dust farming. The local gas station at the edge, near the highway, sold these books – kind of like those old Mexican comic books you used to get in Tijuana, only these were about dreams and mystical powers instead of sex. How you could dream things into being, and change reality, including – if the books were to be taken seriously – things like rain. People joked about them and gave Bobby, the mechanic who ran the Lucky Star gas station, a fair bit of grief for having them.

But they still bought them, no matter what they said to Bobby. Everyone bought the books when they all thought nobody else could see. You could tell; it was in the way their eyes darted to and fro like hummingbirds under glass and in the sound of their laughter – high and too fast, the way you do when it really isn't funny. People bought those books from Bobby, jokes or not.

And across the town, people read those books, desperately hoping and hoping. Every night they read them, just like they bought new ones when there were new ones to be had. Every night they read, down in the secret dark where fears and wishes wrestle almost indistinguishable from one another. Every night they would pray and beg, dreaming fitfully of rain with teeth clenched.

And every day, the sky held, and the dust rolled on.

At some point, I moved away to Dallas, and what I viewed then as civilization. Time passed after I left, as time does. I lengthened my bones and traded the thoughts of a child for those of a serious adult, though not entirely willingly. Like a good many adults whose childhoods weren't always a source of familiar comfort, I attempted to place the usual distances. I almost never called, and always managed to conveniently be too busy to visit.

I took a job that involved some traveling, though none of the sort that involved either wild adventure or great distances. Most of them were within the tristate area and eastward, until an assignment came about that sent me westward, placing my childhood hometown very near my travel path. As I reviewed the intended route, I tried to recall the last time I had been there and realized that I could not. A growing unease fell over me as I then tried to remember the last time I had spoken with my parents, and could not remember that, either.

The night before my trip found me staring at my phone several times throughout the evening before deciding not to call. I would just stop by. I was not entirely sure why I felt this need, or this unease, but my plan seemed logical enough: stop by, say hello, do whatever visiting necessary to allay the uneasy feeling. Use the excuse of work as a means to avoid staying any time beyond the needed.

I drove westward and northward, through towns barely big enough to be on maps, named for past things or peoples that not even the few remaining residents remember the stories for. I drove onward, against a seemingly unchanging landscape, under unyielding skies, until I saw the sign for Bobby's old Lucky Star gas station, ever watchful at exit 88, and turned off the highway.

I had but hardly stepped out of the car and into the store when a voice drifted slowly from behind the counter in greeting.

I always figured you'd be back by one of these days, said Bobby – for it was indeed he – whether you knew it or not, can't say. But here you are.

I squinted as I stepped into the store, trying to adjust between the harsh sun outside and the single dying fluorescent light that Bobby favored for illumination. I noticed that Bobby's back was to me, with no indication that he'd ever turned to look at the door.

I started to ask how he knew it was me, but Bobby cut me off – Before you even ask, there's a mirror. It's always been there, just like I have. As for how I knew it was you, after all this time? Things don't change as much as maybe you think they do or should. Not the important ones, anyhow. Think on that before asking anything else, maybe – all this said without turning around. I shut my mouth before anything else could escape and went back to the car to drive into town and to think on what Bobby meant by that.

It must have been Bobby's words that caused some sort of tunnel vision as I drove to my parents' house; a dimness in perception that did not fade until the final echoes of my knocking for the fourth time faded. Then and only then did I see the dust skirling around my feet, as it blew up little puffs, up and down the empty street, hopping back and forth between drifts built over years. The dust did its best to hitch a ride as I ran back to my car, chased by silence, heading for the Lucky Star with far too many questions to fit in my mouth comfortably.

But all those questions never left my lips; I had left a place of questions only to return to somewhere from which all answers had fled.

The door to the Lucky Star stood slightly ajar and swung open as I walked up, feet gritting on the dust of uncounted years. There was no answer to my call out and no sign of anyone having been there for decades. Motes swirled and danced under the fitful light of that one florescent light that held on somehow, a forgotten nightlight. Only a box of those dream books still behind the counter, that crumbled into nothing when I touched them, gave any sign that Bobby had been there...or that there ever was a Bobby to begin with.

I returned to my car and began the journey home, lips pressed tightly together, to keep the dust from spilling out.

Author's Note:

One can, I suppose, make any kind of argument for the literary nature (and, by extension, influence) of a story. The roots of it, so to speak. This one comes in part from a mild fascination with magical realism – that genre of fiction where the real world and the magical spend a fair amount of time do-si-do-ing each other – which accounts for the slightly ethereal spin on places I know well from my own personal history.

I presented this one at a literary conference panel discussion during my junior year of college. The most popular question, right after "Was the Lucky Star real?" was, "I'm not sure I get it, can you explain?"

3

Them Old Familiar Drive-in Blues

A trip to the Orbit (ex post facto). Monsters, possible danger, but at least no bad country music.

G oddamn, I love the movies. You might even say I was made for the movies. I don't mean to be in them or anything like that; I've got the wrong kind of face for that. Not saying I'm ugly or nothing, but more that I don't have a face that folks pay attention to. The kind of face that when handing you your change, the cashier girl always looks right past, even if there ain't nothing behind but the same stuff in the store you know she looks at so much, probably sees it in her dreams. Not forgettable, though, because to forget means you had to remember in the first place, and I don't get that far.

Having that kind of face doesn't exactly spell future movie star, though I guess I could always go be one of them extras if ever my feelings got hurt enough to warrant it. Movies always need extras – crowds, corpses, or whatever and don't care what you do or don't look like. This lack of bankability hasn't never dampened my love of movies though. One might even say it's the opposite effect: knowing I'll never be faced with the pressure of actually being in one frees me to enjoy them all the more.

And how I do; while it would not be totally inaccurate to say that I love pretty much all things cinematic and will watch almost anything, I feel that some qualifiers must be allowed for. I'll watch anything except musicals. Can't stand those – way too damn silly, with people breaking into song when they should be doing something else – fighting, fucking, even laundry. So, anything except musicals. This is not to say that I don't have favorites though, because everyone has those. You ever meet someone who tells he doesn't, you know he's either lying or the most unconcerned, agreeable sonofabitch who ever lived. He might be just that, but all the same, I wouldn't lend him any money, should I happen to have any. Everybody has favorites. Mine are horror movies (the bloodier and sleazier the better) and cult movies, because well, because. Who doesn't love them a comedy about cannibals?

Growing up in a big city like Dallas, and being possessed of both a love of movies and a lack of a future in them, I had my run of theaters to indulge in. From the megaplexes with thirty screens of first-runs to the tiny arthouses showing nothing but foreign films (and that always reeked of unwashed people and shitty home-rolled cigarettes), I had a wide-open field, and could see anything I wanted, any way I wanted. 35mm, 70mm wide, IMAX, 3D, you name it, I could see anything.

Well, almost anything.

The one thing I could not see was a drive-in, because there weren't any in town. Well, any *left* in town, I really should say. There was one once, but it burnt down before I could start driving. Given that it was showing Howard the Duck at the time of its demise, I can't rightly say that this was not totally unprecedented or unwarranted because, goddamn, that movie sucked. Anyhow, the Comet Twin went up in flames right during a dazzling display of Howard's Quack-Fu and was never rebuilt. I heard the owners moved to Florida or died, but as that's neither here nor there, I guess the details aren't important. What is is that no new drive-in theaters got built, leaving me without that experience.

Until today.

I'd heard about the Orbit for years now: a legendary drive-in theater off Interstate 45, in the wilds beyond Dallas, but before you got to anywhere civilized, like Houston. Stories went, the Orbit was known for its wild weekend triple-feature All-Night Horror Show – slasher films, creature features, and such like. All the kind of stuff someone with tastes like mine would have more than a few dreams over. Way folks talked about the place, you'd think the concession girls were all centerfolds, and would give you a handy with your cherry Coke, or at least genuinely smile at you like they meant it. The Orbit was Heaven, or at least parked close enough to hit it with a rock, and not all that much arm behind it.

Or so the stories went anyhow. I'd also heard some crazy stuff happened there a year or so ago that led to the theater shutting down. Depending on who you talked to, there was an incident with bikers or gangs that caused the shutdown. Others said it was a tornado or electrical storm. Few folks said it was aliens, but nobody took that very seriously, as those saying it were the type who thought aliens caused everything from the last slice of pizza vanishing to crop circles and well, you just can't take those folks seriously. Even if they're right, you just can't.

Regardless of the real reason behind it, the Orbit was in fact closed – that I had on good authority. I had also heard it had been recently acquired and was about to start the process of rehab and renovation for an as of yet undetermined future reopening date. In the meantime, the Orbit still stood as it was following the events of that night – a strange and watchful cinematic presence, lurking in the darkness off I-45, blue and white Orbit sign still magically lit.

Or so the stories went, anyhow. Nobody seemed to know exactly.

All I knew was that there was a currently abandoned drive-in theater outside of town with mysterious and conflicting stories on what happened, lights that never went out and that I had to see it.

There was only one way to know for sure, so I gassed up my truck and headed down to see what I could see.

It was approaching twilight when I pulled into the Orbit lot; I'd left plenty early but still managed to get here later than I had intended due to several wrecks. First thing I noticed was that the light wasn't on on the Orbit sign, but I figured maybe it was due to the sun still being kinda up, and not just one of them urban legend story details. Wasn't a big deal really; plenty of light still left to see, and I had thought to get a flashlight at Love's. I got out and started walking around, shining my flashlight and trying to look like I belonged there and not like some trespassing dumbass with the kind of excuse that would just about beg for extra jail time if caught.

First thing I noticed was the mess. No matter what the story was on what happened here, there had been a lot of people there that weekend and things ended abruptly. There weren't a ton of empty abandoned cars to make the Orbit have this weird Mary Celeste vibe or anything, but all the same, you got the feeling like shit here went bad and everyone just went away. I wandered deeper into the second lot, old popcorn bags and some leftover paper bats swirling around my feet. Though long since emptied of people for...some reason, the place still had a weird odor hanging over it – a kind of funky, musty smell of old popcorn, soda syrup, old sex musk (this IS a drive-in after all), shit and...ozone. If Hell had public bathrooms, they'd probably smell like Lot B of the Orbit.

I had just realized that the whitish stuff around my feet was a mixture of what looked to be ashes and some weird-looking popcorn when I heard a crashing noise off to my right, followed by a roar with a lot of angry bass, like Godzilla woke up from a night on the couch with a bad hangover to find Mrs. Godzilla fucking the plumber. Because I have seen more than my share of horror movies (I did mention I love movies and was made for this, right?) I did **not** turn around to see what it was responsible for the sound but instead opted to run like hell (silently or at least as close as you get when running because screaming gets you killed. Horror movies, remember?) for my truck over in Lot A.

I made it to the truck, but the fucking thing would not start. In fact, I'm still sitting in the sonofabitch right now. Power comes on when I turn the key over okay enough, but it just won't go, like something's holding me in place. While I got power, I do not have radio – not even static. Probably just as well; radio out here in the spaces between towns can be pretty shitty. Last thing I think I'd want is to be eaten by some fucking monster from another dimension to the strains of "There's A Tear In My Beer" or "All My Ex's Live in Texas" or something like that. I mean, yeah, I'm still dying in a terrible way, being eaten, but there are limits to how terrible that should be.

But it's not the source of the noise or if I will turn around and look at it when or if it gets here to eat me (pretty sure I will be unable to avoid doing this. Don't lie, you would too.) that I find my thoughts turning to. No, for some goddamn reason, it's the popcorn I can't seem to stop thinking about. It was everywhere (not that unusual, this is a theatre), and it was **still** there after all this time (okay, maybe a little bit unusual) – I waded through mounds of it during my explorations. But it's not even the fact that there was still popcorn here after all this time that is stuck like a splinter in my brain. Hell, it's not even that I thought I could hear a voice faintly as I walked around through the mess – "chuckachew, chuckachew chew" or some such bullshit like that – none of those things.

What I cannot seem to let go of – even with the thought of something unknown and potentially huge/angry/ravenous – is this:

Know how I said that popcorn looked kinda weird? Well, I kinda fibbed a bit. I picked up a handful when I was walking around in it, trying to figure out how the hell there could still be any popcorn after all this time. Turned a couple of popped kernels over in my hand, and goddamned if they didn't have, well...a fuckin' *eye* in the center.

But really, I think it's the fact that one of those fuckers *winked* at me – guess that's the part I can't let go of.

Author's Note:

I'll dispense with any customary preamble and get down to it – this one here owes its genesis to Joe R. Lansdale, and the Orbit Drive-In theater of *The Drive-In* fame. Readers of Lansdale (my own self being one, of course) would have picked up on this right away. That said, I just thought I should be clear – cover all bets and bases, if you will.

It was around the time that *The Drive-In: Multiplex* was announced as a thing that was going to be that I got to thinking: "Dang. Those were pretty fun reads, and that Orbit sounded badass. Maybe not so much what happened to them dudes but still. And now there's a bunch of stories coming out set in that shared universe. I wonder if I could write one."

So, I did.

This is the result.

I (very) briefly toyed with the idea of seeing if some of the awesome folks who contributed to Multiplex (and whom, by the magic powers of today's so-called social media, I interact with) would perhaps read it. In the end though I kinda chickened out and didn't send it to any of 'em.

Not even Keith, who is nice enough to have lunch with me occasionally.

Hope y'all like it.

4

EVIL

A Travelogue

You ever wonder if some places are just bad? I don't mean bad like they got shitty schools or bad jobs or anything like that; I mean bad, like bad things happen there, with an outsized frequency. You know, what some people would call evil, or whatever.

Like it's in the water, or the air of the place, touching everything in it.

In its blood, if you will.

As one could probably imagine, there's hardly a consensus on this. Some people say yea, sure, some places just are, it's plain to see; others, nay – that's just a speculative feeling with no hard science to back it. And to be fair, the nay voices have a point: there is no hard science to back it. Data, sure – there's observable data if one looks. But nothing one can point out and say, "yeah, some places are given to bad things, and here's why."

Still, provable or not, it's something that I turn over in my head, especially when driving around town. This place has seen more than the average share of terrible things, if one looks closely – everything from the expected domestic violence or arson to the one they're calling the Twilight Trail Killer in the papers. It's enough to make a person wonder if some places aren't somehow magnets for such things.

Take the Watkins house over on Norway Road, over in the North Side, for example.

It's well enough known – hell, it's a matter of Dallas public record – that old man Watkins had that place built in 1926, and that there were more than a handful of tragic events with its construction. A couple of workers died; one when a section of roofing unexpectedly gave way, and the other a heart attack due to the high heat of that summer. It's rumored that Watkins' miserliness and insistence on tight schedules contributed to that one, as he was known not to pay anyone who he thought "took too many breaks" while working for him.

That's all in the papers of the times, and easy enough to look up. What's less talked about, but no less true for that, is how Watkins' niece disappeared from the backyard and never heard from again. Oh, I know what you're thinking – how are worker deaths newsworthy and the disappearance of a child from a wealthy family not? A fair enough question, but money is money for one. That and the circumstances of little Millicent Watkins' disappearance were just strange enough that the family buried any word, for fear of scandal. They hushed it all, and sold the house, never breathing a word to the buyers.

However, if the note Travis Jameson – the fella who bought the property – left behind in his safe before torching the place, then something very dark indeed happened to that little girl. Oh sure, it's entirely possible that Jameson himself was not entirely right in the head. Still, lines like "I hear her voice, speaking in the earth" do make a person wonder, especially if he doesn't know the history.

About a mile west from the Watkins place is Old Garson Park, the site of the first known victim of the Twilight Trail Killer, Shelly Barker, a waitress who lived over in Lochwood. Based on the park's location and the victim's work and home, police assumed it was a random dump.

Continuing westward past the park is Marsh Lane; a bit past that and there's a subdivision marked by silly streets with names like Princess, Lancelot, and Valiant – frivolous stuff. The houses there aren't necessarily what one would call new, but new enough, I guess. They've been there since redevelopment began back in the early Eighties during a boom period. While new in terms of the city itself, they've been around long enough to help people forget about the asylum that used to occupy this part, back when this was the edge of town, and things out here were less seen and even less thought about.

The asylum's been gone some time now and all that remains are the whispered stories of what supposedly happened there – accounts of abuse, illegal experiments, and other unsavory things – the kind that likely swirl around all such places. It was reportedly shut down due to those atrocities and destroyed in hopes of burying the past. In accordance with such stories, the land where Winfield Home stood is supposedly forever marked by those damaged lives.

Whether or not any of these evil things happened at Winfield remains largely the stuff of rumor and urban legend; never as famous (or rather, infamous) as Timberlawn or as documented, it's a place that few remember. It could indeed just be a myth, a spooky story, with nothing more than the desire to scare to power it. The outsized number of violent crimes for this particular area suggests otherwise, though, and that the deeds of the past can't just be hidden under wishful thinking or storybook rebranding.

The second and third victims of the Twilight Trail Killer were found several miles to the south of the former asylum grounds, over in the park surrounding Bachman Lake. Though found together in the park, further examinations revealed a week's gap in time of death for Lily Warrington and DeeDee Saunders, the two victims. Police remain unsure of any relationship between the two women.

Now, you might be thinking, well, okay, these all sound bad, but they don't sound all that unusual. Like, these are the kinds of things one might expect to hear about from a big city – sordid tales of violence, the weakness of human nature, and things of that sort. I'm not even saying you'd be wrong in thinking that, mind you. Far from it. Every city has its scars, and under every scar is a story. Dig deep enough or far enough, and you'll likely find the monster or the tragedy that made that scar.

So, I can understand why you might think that way. I do.

Consider this, however, as we come further to Harry Hines Boulevard. I'm sure you, like everyone else in this city, know its reputation, and the sorts of people one finds here. From school children to the mayor, this particular stretch is well-known. Everyone has stories or has heard stories.

Did you know, however, that back in 1980, the Dallas Police Department was aware of not one, not two, but *four* suspected serial killers operating in this five-block strip? Or that of these four, only one was apprehended, and then in relation to something unrelated? Even then, the one that was picked up was almost let go...until he decided to confess to the murders on the strip, as well as others.

Maybe the police didn't care and preferred to let it happen, maybe even glad they died. Or perhaps they did care, but just accepted it as "something about that part of town."

To the west, just under the highway over there, is Crown Park, where they found the body of Kate Briggs. At 72, she was the oldest known victim of the Twilight Trail Killer. Initially suspected as perhaps being more personal to the Twilight Trail Killer due to age discrepancy, this theory has yet to gain anything else to substantiate it.

From Crown Park it's a little bit of a stretch down Royal Lane – a misnomer, as can be clearly seen – to get back to the east side of town. Judging by the dubious-looking shops, seedy convenience stores and check cashing places, any kind of majesty this road might have once had has since been forgotten. These days it's just another connection between the not-so-nice west side and the slightly nicer east, as reflected in the shift from rundown businesses to minor denomination churches and small parks as the road unwinds.

None of the Twilight Trail Killer's known victims have been found further west than Crown Park, or further east than Flag Pole Hill, near the lake. Police experts have stated that this is indicative of someone likely local, given the intimate familiarity with the city's parks, and deliberate arrangement of each body.

Just north of the lake's park is another subdivision with lighthearted street names – animals, mostly, like Deer Trail or Eagle Trail – that match the unassuming houses that line them. A fairly typical-looking neighborhood, with houses on the larger side of middle, though nothing ostentatious. No luxury cars fill the driveways; there's little to suggest that anything more than the morning paper delivery happens here.

Certainly nothing to suggest a history of violence, drugs or murder for hire. Yet all three occurred within the walls of 7834 Blackbird Lane – that one on the corner there, currently unoccupied – back in 1985. A prominent local attorney apparently lured a couple to this house, supposedly to coerce drug money owed. Though conflicting stories emerged as to exactly how things transpired, the results were unambiguous, both victims bludgeoned and stabbed repeatedly.

Neighbors heard the screams and noises inside the house, but assumed it was a domestic dispute that they didn't need to be involved in. When interviewed, all attested to the attorney's overall character, appearing both shocked and surprised over his involvement with drugs and a double homicide. His confession, however, sealed the deal, and the house was taken back by the bank when the attorney went to prison. Whether the notoriety or just the general proximity to the lake helped sell it, can't really say – but sell it did, and quickly, to an out-of-state couple who couldn't believe their seemingly good fortune. They moved in that following summer.

They were found four months later, the pileup of mail and newspapers having become large enough to prompt someone to check. There was little mention of it in the papers, and officially it was marked as murder-suicide. But the way the stories in the neighborhood go, no weapons were recovered, and the message left behind on the wall in blood – one that was quickly removed by the police – seemed like no suicide note.

It's changed hands a few times in the decades since, selling but never for very long. It's still vacant, though there's no sign out in front to indicate its availability. People still cross to the other side of the street, to avoid walking in front of it. Given how many years have passed, it makes one wonder if they know the history, or just sense something strange about the place.

Though known in the local media as the Twilight Trail Killer, no evidence has been shown to indicate that the park trails are anything more than public dumping spots. None of the parks used show any signs of either victim or killer having been there prior to body discovery. Despite the usage of well-visited parks, there remain no witnesses, leaving the precise timing and placement of the victims' bodies – on an open public trail at twilight, with death occurring only a few minutes beforehand – a complete mystery. Runner Jane Wallace, upon discovering the Twilight Trail Killer's seventh victim, Ann-Marie Butler, on the part of the White Rock Trail near Pelican Point, recalls the utter shock, noting that's "it's an area with a lot of visibility in all directions" and that she "should have seen something or someone, given how the body just appeared" but did not.

Aside from the usage of local parks and body arrangement – the bodies being placed so that the victim's left-hand points precisely to the constellation of Scorpio, regardless of day – there is little else to suggest much for pattern or victimology. The victims thus far have all been women, but that appears to be the only link, as there are no common denominators across age, race or social background. There has been no evidence that the victims had any relationship or connection.

A little further south and east leads out of the lake. A little further up Buckner is what was known as "The Scientology House," before it burned down a few years ago. Built in the 1940s, it was something of an architectural were-creature: party mansion, cult religion celebrity center, rental property, and finally derelict, rotting away in obscurity. Uninhabited for years, save the occasional transient looking for shelter or kids exploring, it mysteriously burned down on a clear spring afternoon. No clear signs of arson were found, and per the owner of the property, it had no occupants. However, the bloodstains and strange symbols found scrawled into the flooring suggested that someone or something had been there, before the fire.

There's a small park on the opposite side of the street and around the bend from where the Scientology House stood. None of the Twilight Trail Killer's victims have turned up there, but it's been reported that the police have it under surveillance, along with other parks, as a precaution. It, along with Ferguson Park further south, is under watch along with the others until the Twilight Trail Killer is caught, or the murders are determined to be over.

They sound confident – the police – but I don't know if I share that. As you might have guessed, some pretty dark things have happened here, and easily. Like it's just made for it, or something.

I can tell that you're awake and aware enough, even if you can't move easily just yet. I mean, even if I didn't calculate or know exactly when that sedative that I gave you would wear off, I've been around long enough to know when someone's truly out and when they're playing possum. Bodies move differently, you know – alive, asleep, and dead, they move differently. You don't have to keep your eyes closed, you know.

We're almost to where we were going. I just thought you might like to see a little of the sights – get a little of the backstory, so to speak. Make it a bit more interesting. But we're almost here, and it will be over soon. See that park up ahead there?

Oh, I know. I know. You're scared. You're thinking maybe you can get the window down, scream loudly, someone will help if they hear you. Maybe someone will even – hear that is, if you're loud enough.

But I wouldn't go expecting much good to come from that. Places like here – you know, bad places, *evil* places – they're just not set up that way.

Author's Note:
Like another story in this collection (the Lansdalean "Cosmic Drive-In Blues"), this one can trace some parentage of sorts to another story, albeit a bit more obliquely. Unlike that one, "Evil" isn't set in anyone else's universe, or anything like that. In this case, it's more that I read Peter Straub's "A Short Guide to The City" (included in *Houses Without Doors*) and thought that the idea of an unsettling travelogue was just too cool. Some of the places and incidents referenced may be familiar, though I will of course say they aren't necessarily real.

Not all of them, anyhow.

5

SOMETIMES THE ORDER OF WORDS DOES MATTER

This is all Brian's fault. I know, maybe not the most helpful thing to say, especially given the current circumstances, but it's true. Should we (or, if being totally honest, *when*) we all end up dead, I want whoever it is that reads this to know.

It was all Brian's fault.

It all started off normally enough; an afternoon with the guys – David, Joe, and of course, Brian. We were doing our usual Sunday afternoon routine of eating pizza and watching horror movies, with the occasional ad-libbing of lines or comments on the visual effects. Typical stuff. Normal stuff. *Routine* stuff.

Joe had just given his best impression of Bill Moseley's Chop-Top from *Texas Chainsaw Massacre 2*, when Brian let out a low whistle and motioned for us to come over. He held up the issue of *Scream* he'd been flipping through and pointed to an ad in the back.

It was an ad for something labeled "Killer Zombie Assault Van," replete with pictures of a van tricked out for what would ostensibly be surviving a zombie apocalypse. Brian was pretty taken with the idea of somehow acquiring this. Of the four of us, he was the biggest fan of the genre, and could quote not just *Night*, but *Day* and *Dawn of the Dead*, line for line. His interest was piqued, and I sensed that the other two were intrigued as well. It *was* a pretty sweet-looking van, and I would be lying if I didn't feel a minor thrill as well.

However, something about the ad and its wording kept bugging me. Brian just shrugged, passing it off as English maybe not being the ad poster's first language.

I could see it in his eye, and the eyes of the others, that this was something they were set on. So, I told myself I was overthinking it and let it pass.

We checked our pooled resources, and responded to the ad. A week later, it was delivered and sat, blackly sinister, outside Brian's house for us to admire. From its flat black paint to its reinforced grille and gunports, this van all but shouted for us to get inside, if we wanted to survive. We'd seen the movies, read the magazines, and played the games. We knew how this was supposed to go. We got inside and turned the key hanging from the ignition.

The engine roared to life, a low, throaty hum. And then everything went sideways.

We were checking out the interior and noting the customizations (buttons labeled "Weapons System," "Lockdown Mode," and other features) when we heard what sounded like a low growling coming from outside. At first, I assumed it was just the engine, so I turned the key to stop it and save some gas.

But the sound didn't die with the engine. If anything, it was louder. So, I looked out the rear blackout window to see if I could get a fix on the source of the noise.

And that's how I discovered that we were, for all practical purposes, trapped in a van and surrounded by what appeared to be a horde of hungry zombies, intent on consuming us.

I backed away from the window, unsure of what to do or say. I was still sorting that out when Joe decided to have a look for himself. He peered through the side vent, saw the zombies, and proceeded to pass out in fright. This inability to process forced my hand a bit in telling David and Brian just what it was outside. In hopes of not duplicating Joe's reaction, I tried to be as optimistic as one can when faced with imminent destruction at the hands of malevolent undead cannibals.

I was half successful.

I say half, because neither fainted. However, as they both went into a state of shock and denial over this, the mere fact that they were still conscious wasn't as much a win as I'd initially hoped. After some screaming and futile punching of the "Weapons System" button, Brian slumped in the driver's seat, either unwilling or unable to open his eyes to see anything else. David, while technically still conscious, kept muttering to himself, unresponsive to anything else I said, leaving me the only one still functioning in the van.

The growling is getting louder. I have little doubt that before long, the zombies will figure a way to break into here, if by no other means than dumb brute force. I mean, for all the fancy "customizations" and paint, the reality is that this is just a regular old van. A regular old van that we – all of us, including me – will likely be dragged out of and subsequently eaten.

How did this come to pass, you wonder? By coincidence, this is also the last thing Brian said before retreating into his slump of denial, eyes bugging out of his head. How is this even happening?

I'll be the first to admit – I am no scientist. Shit, I failed high school biology twice. However, I don't think what's happening here is exactly a science problem as it is a language problem.

The language of the ad description – "Killer Zombie Assault Van" – I can't help but think this is why. Even now, with death approaching, I can't shake the feeling that maybe, just maybe, a "Killer Zombie Assault Van" would be something that *summons* killer hordes of zombies, instead of a "Zombie Killer Assault Van," made for the elimination of zombie hordes.

Sometimes, the order of words *does* matter.

I know, I know – we all read the ad. We all pooled our money, and we all bought this van that we are all going to die in. We made this happen.

But this is still all your fault, Brian.

Author's Note:

This one has some very far-reaching roots. My mother, a former English professor, was something of what people jokingly call a "grammar Nazi" and, pretty prescriptive about her views on what she thought was the correct way of speaking. I of course, relished challenging this, often steering conversations on the subject into "well, why does it *have* to be that way" and other similar lines of questioning on why things are said or phrased the way they are.

Maybe not the nicest thing ever, but – deliberate chain jerking aside – I did want to know.

Flash-forward some years, and we end up with an older me still pondering not only *why*, but *what* the practical implications of word order and choice could be.

With zombies.

6

HARMADILLOS II

The Night, Rainey Street and Thee

I t's late Saturday night – really more Sunday morning – when Brian and I pour ourselves out of Container Bar, intent on stumbling our way back to where he's parked, over at the Four Seasons. Given the niceness of the night and our combined level of intoxication, we opt for a stroll along the Colorado river, in the name of safety. After all, Brian says as he takes my arm to guide me onto the footpath near the river's edge, how embarrassing would that be if you came to visit and got run over by some soccer mom in a Suburban? Or worse, a developer in one of those ridiculous new Tesla Cybertruck things. At this, we both laugh and continue down the trail.

"Speaking of such, uh, gruesome sorts of things, is there anything to that Rainey Street Killer thing? You know, all those guys being found in the lake and whatnot? I read an article about that in the Statesman or the Chronicle or somewhere, I think." Brian grimaces and gives me a look. "Not sure where you would have read that, as I'm pretty sure neither one of those publications want to be on record saying there's a serial killer. Yeah, might do something for circulation numbers but you must have read that somewhere else."

"That's not an answer, Brian. Do you think there's any substance to the story?"

Brian snorts. "Nah. The "truth" is that it's a bunch of clumsy drunks who lose their footing, fall in, and drown because, again, they're drunk. As you might have already observed, the banks of Lady Bird Lake here can be pretty slippery. C'mon this way and mind your step some."

"Lady Bird Lake? Is that what this is called?" I ask. Brian grunts, already losing interest in the subject, "Yeah, I guess so." There's a brief pause, and then he asks,

"Hey! Wanna grab a couple ranch waters back at the hotel bar before you turn in?"

"Ranch water?"

Brian snickers. "Yeah, Topo Chico and tequila. Don't scoff 'till you try one. They're good."

"Oh, well, okay I guess."

We head on down the path, carefully picking our way toward our destination, when there's a rustling in the brush to my left. I stop in my tracks, trying to determine exactly where the noise was coming from and what was making it. I'm about to pass it off as a breeze when I spy movement. Getting in closer, I see a very strange looking creature. "Hey! What's this little guy? Kinda looks like an armored possum or something, only much cuter."

From over my shoulder I hear, "Wooooooooowheeee! That lil guy is an armadillo. Got 'em all over the state. They eat bugs and dig holes mostly. What, never seen one before? Don't they have those where you live?"

"No, Brian. We don't. Possums, yes; these guys, no. Maybe they're a Texas thing?" For someone so technically skilled and smart, Brian really did not seem to know much about things outside of his own immediate bubble, including wildlife. I watch the armadillo root around in the leaves, presumably looking for bugs.

"Cute lil dude, ain't he?" Brian's voice suddenly drops lower. "Wanna see something really funny?"

Without even waiting for an answer, he suddenly charges into the bushes, arms extended. Startled, the armadillo makes a noise somewhere between a scream and a squawk, leaping into the air as though jet-propelled before landing back in the pile of leaves it had been rooting through.

Brian is doubled-up, wheezing with laughter. Though mildly horrified, I find myself laughing as well, because it was in fact funny.

However, as the startled creature dashes away from its tormentor, the bushes rustle again, only louder. I look up to see what looks like a trio of glowing red eyes, peering at us through the leaves. As the brush parts, I see what looks like more armadillos emerge, only these are larger, and less cute. We freeze in place, and for a moment, it feels like time has stopped, it's so quiet.

I'm turning to Brian to say, "Maybe we should back away," when the largest and closest of the armadillos suddenly curls into a tight ball and careens towards us so quickly it's a blur. As it collides with Brian's leg, pitching him face forward into the ground, the other two veer off in tandem, seeming to bounce upward as they crash into an old and rotting cypress. There's a cracking noise, followed by a scream as the shattered and heavy tree limb drops on Brian.

I can feel my blood turning to ice as I run, plunging blindly back towards my hotel. As I run, I tell myself that the noises I hear are Brian getting up and away from... whatever those things were, and that he's fine. I tell myself this is all fine and that I must hurry back – I fly home tomorrow. Brian will be okay, I think as I run. He's a fit man. He'll make it. But I don't look back to see.

Later that morning, I'm sitting in my assigned seat for the plane ride back home to Raleigh, scrolling through my social media feeds, when I spot the following headline: "Another body found in Lady Bird Lake," and I feel my throat start to close up. I don't want to tap the "More" button for fear of what I will find but cannot stop myself from reading on.

"The body of Brian Turner, 29, entrepreneur and founder of Cyber HG Group, was found in the shallow waters of the Colorado River known as Lady Bird Lake in downtown Austin by a runner out for an early morning jog. There are no signs of foul play, and the state of the body, along with the broken cypress branches found nearby, suggest an accidental death by misadventure. Further details as to cause, and a full report from the medical examiner's office are still pending."

There's a bit more, but I can't read it. As the words blur together, my blood is again replaced with ice. I think about pressing the button to ask for a blanket, but stop halfway, knowing it will be no use.

7

IT'S INEVITABLE

Ted, Part 1

I t's another boring Saturday afternoon in a series of boring afternoons in the world's most boring vacation ever. My head's been bothering me since the morning, so I'm sitting in my room, restlessly waiting for it to pass.

Fucking Texas. All the way here, I'd heard pretty much nonstop about how hot it was, how it was a perpetual summer, full of sunny days and clear skies. Like Florida or California, but with funnier accents. Guess nobody told whoever's in charge of the weather in this stupid place though, because it's been raining pretty much since we got here. If not for randomly meeting this kid named Steve that day I got dragged to see the stupid Alamo, this would be the worst vacation of all.

Steve's cool though. A little younger than me, and usually not the kind of kid I would pal with. But we share similar interests, which helps with how otherwise lame this place is.

It's finally stopped raining, and I'm trying to decide if I want to go out to find something to burn off the boredom, when suddenly there's a knock at my door.

"Teddy, are you in there?"

Before I can draw another breath, let alone say, yeah I'm here, did you SEE me leave or anything else, there comes another knock and another inquiry.

"Teddy? Hello?"

Teddy. Fuck. If there's anything, I mean *anything*, that I hate as much as being disturbed for nothing, or being asked a lot of dumb questions, it's being called Teddy. You'd think I permanently wore footy pajamas, or sucked my thumb, being called that. Just thinking the name makes me want to puke. Fuckin' Teddy. That's the name of an asswipe who gets his lights punched out, and milk money stolen. A scrubby dipshit. No thanks.

I think for a second about not answering, but quickly let that go. As much as I know that would irritate her, I know it'll just keep the shit going and prolong the agony. The silent treatment is shit you read in books. In real life, it never works.

So, instead, I clear my throat and say, yeah Ma—er, I mean, yeah, I'm in here. My sister's voice outside the door suddenly cycles up: "What did you say?" Cursing myself for the momentary slip, I yell back, "Nothin, nothin. I mean, yeah, yeah – I'm in here. Been here all day. Gotta headache. What do you need?"

Outside my door, her voice came louder – "Don't you get that tone with me, Teddy. You know I don't like it when you do." My head is starting to seriously pound now, like it's going to split; the last thing I want is to talk about, well, anything. I don't think I can take that much more of her, yelling outside my door, or worse, wanting to come in here and talk. I might scream if she does.

So, thinking fast, I grit my teeth and say, "I'm sorry, didn't mean to be rude. What is it?" in the most sincere voice I can muster up.

"That's better."

She's still outside the door and not barging in so yeah, guess that is better. It would be perfect if she would just go away now, and my head would quit doing its best impression of a cracking egg. Still, I'll take it. Can't win all the time, I guess.

It's quiet for a minute, and I'm thinking maybe she's changed her mind about whatever it was. Then, from the other side of the door, I hear "Teddy, I want to talk to you about these pictures I found." shattering that brief hope.

Pictures? What pictures? I'm confused and trying to think what pictures these could be, when she continues.

"I found some pictures. In your room. Under your mattress."

Oh. Oh shit. Those pictures. Shit, shit, *shit*. Should have known they'd bite me. Should have fucking known. My heart sits in my throat, huge as a boulder, as I think of what I should say. Shit.

"You *know* I don't like that kind of stuff and you *know* I won't have that kind of...filth...in this house. Now what do you have to say to that?"

I'm cursing myself for being so careless. How could I have been so sloppy? It's here that panic really starts to hit me; not only does she sound really pissed, but there's a note of suspicion that I really, really do not like. This is really, really, *really* not good. The last thing I want is for her to come in here. I look around frantically, trying to make sure there's nothing else, as I prepare myself for this almost certainty.

I'm still searching, looking for any last-minute thing, when she knocks again, louder. It sounds like she's pounding the door off its hinges, and I think I can almost see it coming loose.

"Teddy? I'm waiting. If you think I'm just gonna go away, think again, mister. What do you have to say for yourself?"

Fuck! Would she please, please, *please* just stop with that fucking name?! It makes me so mad I can hardly see, let alone think. I feel like screaming, and for a second, I almost *do*, even though she's got me dead to rights here. But right as I open my mouth to likely seal my fate, something in the corner catches my eye. Something not quite right, and not good. It's recognition of just what that something *is* that causes me to snap my mouth shut so fast that I nearly bite my tongue. The shock effectively kills my retort and grants me a second of respite. I suck in my breath and try my best to sound truly penitent.

"I know how you feel, and I don't know why I did that. I know it's wrong and look – I 'm really sorry. It won't happen again. I promise." Of course it won't – I cannot afford to be that careless ever again. She has no idea, but what I am saying is literal truth. Well, some of it, anyhow.

There's silence, and then finally she says, "Okay. This better be the last time I ever find anything like this again, mister. I mean it." And with that, she leaves. I mean, really leaves, footsteps receding, going downstairs and everything.

I sit there, in a near daze for close to five minutes after my sister leaves, when it finally hits me that she really left, and I can move again. That was far, far too close, and sheer sloppiness. Totally unacceptable. Gotta make sure to be more careful next time so my sister... excuse me, my *mother*, doesn't find out.

Yes. My mother. See, for some reason, my grandparents (who we live with) maintain this dumb fiction that my mother is really my sister, and that I do not know this. Only, I *do* know, and someday, everyone will know. I will make sure they do. For now, I play along and maintain the story, but that can't last forever.

Nothing stays buried or out of sight forever. It's always only ever a matter of time. Things always rise to the surface. It's inevitable.

That being said, I really cannot stress enough on how lucky I was just now, with her not coming in here. Had she come in here with those pictures and found what I missed... who knows what would have happened.

Apparently, I forgot a bloodstain from the last time.

Author's Note:
As noted in another story's notes (I mean, maybe you read out of order. I do. If the title of one story sounds cooler, I will, in fact, jump ahead. I don't blame you if you do similarly.) I find serial killers and homicidal people interesting. Maybe not as much as I once did when younger, but still interesting.

(Younger me also liked at one time things like baloney and Yoo-Hoo. Not at the same time though. There *are* limits to gross things...even as a kid.)

The one in this story draws from one a little more famous perhaps than the guys in Toolin'. However, as we see in both cases, no matter the age in question, not even serial killers are immune to less than ideal vacation time.

8

LOST CAT

It was Thursday afternoon when Jim first saw the sign on the southeast corner near the post office. "LOST CAT: Answers to Mr. Bonkers. $5000 reward." in bold black text on a yellow canvas background; mounted on two metal poles, it stretched almost 4 feet across. A picture of a medium-haired cat – presumably Mr. Bonkers – looked on reproachfully from under the text. Jim wondered idly if the cat's reproachful look was for the indignity of being on a sign like that, or having a monetary value assigned to him. "Answers to the name of Mr. Bonkers," he thought. "As if a cat ever answered to anything other than pss pss pss." The sign rippled in the wind, making the cat's face momentarily seem to wink, as Jim drove past the corner. Nearly half a million cats in Dallas, he thought, and these folks are offering five thousand to find this one cat. Some people make no sense.

It wasn't long until the sign on the corner was joined by a second sign – this one less banner-like – in the parking lot of the church down the main road that ran past Jim's neighborhood. A traditional signboard on thin metal poles, this one had a scaled-down version of the message: "LOST CAT. $5000 reward," again with a picture of Mr. Bonkers under the text, though a slightly different one. This one was shot at an angle in such a manner that Jim could not help but feel like the cat's eyes were following him as he drove past. The placement of the sign in a church parking lot struck Jim as hilarious, as if it were trying to suggest a spiritual reward was being offered as well. Or perhaps, he mused, as the sign receded in the rearview mirror, it was a plea for divine assistance. Whichever it is, best of luck, he thought. I'm pretty sure Jesus has his hands full as it is.

The third sign, or rather more a placard, didn't show up until Saturday. The size of a standard poster board, this one was affixed to the fence of the second house on the right on Blackwood Lane, the street that led into Jim's subdivision. A near clone of the one in the lot of the Heavenly Harmony Baptist Church lot, this bit of signage, however, had a more startling than amusing effect. Not only did it feel like Mr. Bonkers' reproachful gaze was moving in closer than he cared for, but Jim could not shake the feeling that this sign was not put up so much as it just *appeared*. He knew for a fact that the Ellisons had two Scottish terriers and were, as far as he could recall, solidly dog people. It seemed unlikely that they would be so cooperative in trying to find this cat, but the sign was there. Jim figured it was just a silly coincidence but decided that maybe his morning walks would have a different path – at least until the sign came down.

Without even being fully aware of it, Jim had altered his daily routines to avoid the lost cat signs that he'd seen to a point where he'd almost forgotten about them. As a result, his discovery of the fourth one, affixed to a telephone pole at the end of his block that connected to Miller Road, jolted him, producing a sense of deepening unease. He knew without turning or looking around that he was alone on the street yet could not shake the feeling that somebody or something was watching him. Jim stared at the flyer stapled to the pole, reduced to an almost accusatory simplicity. No names, just the two words – LOST CAT – and the picture. No further details or mention of the reward. Before he had realized he was doing it, Jim tore the flyer down and wadded it into a ball. He stuffed it deep into his hoodie pocket, and walked quickly back to his house without sparing a backward glance.

The following week, there was heavy construction at Jim's office. This forced him to work from home out of necessity. Between his subconsciously altered daily routine and temporarily increased workload, Jim fell into ordering out for meals, and rarely left home.

The construction project was extended, requiring Jim to work from home for another two weeks. Jim continued with his adapted routine, and the lost cat signs, once so troubling, retreated from his memory.

Until the following Monday.

The construction was now completed, and word had come down to return to the office. Jim was just about to slide behind the wheel of his Camry when he noticed a folded piece of paper under one of the windshield wipers. Curious, he paused and got out to retrieve it. Carefully lifting the wiper, Jim took the paper that had been held in place, unfolded it, and stood still in shock.

"REWARD," it read. No other text. Just that singular word, and a photo of Mr. Bonkers, looking sad.

Jim felt a stab of fear lance through him. How did they get into his garage? What do they want? These thoughts raced.

Jim peered more closely at the paper in his hand and noticed, for the first time, a phone number under the picture. He sighed. I suppose this is it, he thought. I really have no other choice but to call and see. Hopefully, they're still offering a reward. I could sure use that money.

That, and well, Mr. Bonkers' body *is* beginning to smell pretty bad now.

Author's Note:

This one, unlike some others, does more than dip a toe into the real world – in this case, it's more like one, if not both feet planted in reality. Well, more like one solidly and the other waving around, as some liberties were taken. Yes, there really is/was a lost cat in the neighborhood. There were/are signs with reward amounts and a sad looking feline on them; I'd see them pretty much everywhere. Driving to the post office, the grocery store, you name it – there was this lost cat, giving you a reproachful eye.

His name wasn't Mr. Bonkers though.

9

Appearing Nitely

Robert was new to the neighborhood. He'd moved there unexpectedly and, owing to the suddenness of the move, found himself in a smallish house over on the north side of Fort Worth, on Chestnut, with no washer or dryer connections, or even space for the appliances, had there been. This placed Robert in a minor quandary, as he was a rather fastidious sort and did not relish the idea of his new place rapidly filling up with untidy piles of clothing in various states of cleanliness. Clearly, the only solution was to find a suitable laundromat close by. It would also need to be within walking distance, as – again, owing to the unexpected suddenness of his move – Robert no longer had a car. A tall order by most standards, but here, Robert lucked out. There was a BrightKleen Washateria just three blocks down and two streets over – close enough to accomplish the needed task while just far enough to make for a nice walk.

Robert was double-checking to make sure the dryer had not, in fact, eaten one of his socks, when a flyer on the wall to his left caught his eye. It was crookedly taped, and looked to have been handmade, with lettering made from various magazine cutouts, proudly proclaiming, "Appearing Nitely! Diamond Lil, The Texas Jewel at From Scratch Bar & Grill. 9PM. Free show!" No other information, save for the bar's address, appeared on the flyer. Robert located his missing sock (tucked inside a pair of jeans), folded the rest of his laundry, and went home.

Each week, Robert continued to do his laundry at the BrightKleen; each week there would be a new flyer for Diamond Lil taped to the wall. The lettering varied occasionally, and every so often there would be a random bit of art. The text, however, remained the same, with its promise of Diamond Lil "appearing nitely."

Each week, Robert would read the flyer as though considering it before ultimately heading back to his place over on Chestnut. As he walked back, basket at hip, he would think, "Maybe next week I'll go over and check it out."

But he never did.

Until that one night when Robert found himself walking, feeling as though his feet were guided by some other force, not to the BrightKleen but over to Pine, towards From Scratch. He stopped outside the door, suddenly reluctant to continue. Other patrons flowed around him on their way inside, not even sparing a backward glance of curiosity. Robert stood there a minute longer before finally working up the courage to enter. He pushed open the door, warm air redolent with the tang of beer wafting out, and looked around, eyes adjusting to the dimmer interior of the bar. There were no neon lights, or tacky bar signs visible, a minor detail Robert appreciated. He could hear a familiar song playing in the background, the words "There is a party, everyone is there" swirling past his ears as he walked inside. As he looked over the bar, taking it in, it seemed that the barman gave him the tiniest of knowing looks, happening so quickly that Robert remained unsure.

Robert checked his watch. It was ten minutes to nine, the time when Diamond Lil performed, according to the flyer. He looked around for an unoccupied seat, searching for something with a good view that also provided an easy exit if needed. Finally locating an empty booth to the right of the small stage, Robert sat down and waited. Tapping a foot against the edge of his seat, he watched the other bar patrons, mildly envious of them in their unhurried and easy familiarity as he waited for the show to begin.

It then occurred to Robert that he was in a bar, and that he should order something to drink. As he sat there, temporarily lost in an agony of indecision, a spotlight spiked down, illuminating a small circle on the tiny bar stage. The volume of chatter, while never deafening, receded to a hum of indistinction – a singular Barvoice, blurred and buzzing into the background.

It was showtime.

Seeming to coalesce rather than walk into the spotlight, Diamond Lil appeared. From the tiny nod to the band behind her to her precise dance steps, it was easy enough to see that she was a practiced professional who had done this many times before. Yet nothing came across as forced or tired; everything felt fresh. Though he had no prior basis for comparison, Robert was left with the feeling of something being seen for the first time, beyond just his own. Transfixed, he sat there, eyes unable to leave the stage.

Before he knew it, the set drew to a close. Diamond Lil sketched a little wave to the bar and seemed to disappear from the stage in a near reversal of her appearance. Robert blinked. The stage was empty now, save for a stool under the spotlight, as if all that he had witnessed was but a dream. Still feeling the music buzzing as if trapped in his skin, Robert got up out of the booth, and headed to the bar. He didn't really want a drink, but had to talk to someone, anyone, about what he'd witnessed.

Robert threaded his way through the crowd that had swelled during Diamond Lil's set, making his way to the bar. He cleared his throat in expectation of having to speak over the noise, which had risen as the final notes of the show had faded. He was about to shout his order, when the barman interrupted.

"What'll you have, Robert?"

Robert felt his throat close in shock, words and air vanishing. "How...how did you...I mean, how do you," he stumbled, trying to find his footing. "How do you know my name?"

The bartender shrugged, looking unconcerned as he polished a glass. "I dunno. Guess maybe I saw you before or something." He set the glass down next to the others in the line to his right. "Now, what'll it be?"

Robert stared at the bartender. "But I've never been here. Tonight was my first time."

The bartender picked up another glass and started polishing it. "If you say so." He finished with the glass and reached for a bottle. "Maybe you just look like a

Robert to me." He opened the bottle, poured two fingers into one of the newly polished glasses, and slid it across the bar. "Bottoms up, pal."

Robert took the glass and sniffed at it. "How'd you know I liked rye?" The bartender smirked. "Like I said, you look like a Robert to me, and every Robert I've known has liked rye. So, I figured you did, too. A lucky guess." However, the look he gave Robert as he put the bottle back suggested otherwise.

That look, in conjunction with the almost careless delivery, failed to convince and there was a moment of awkward silence as Robert contemplated what to do next. He hesitated, glass in hand, floating in indecision. The bartender leaned closer. "Maybe I'm just really good at my job. Or," he said, drawing the word out. "...maybe I saw your keys dangling out of your jacket pocket. You know, the ones with that fob with your name in script?" He laughed as Robert blinked in confusion. "Oh, if you could just see the look on your face just now. Relax. Drink up." The bartender turned back to the row of glasses behind him, still chuckling.

Robert felt the tips of his ears burning in a wash of equal parts relief and embarrassment over his initial reaction. He took a slug from the glass, grateful for the low mood lighting. Nerves somewhat restored, Robert decided to press forth with his reason for coming up to the bar. "What can you tell me about Diamond Lil?" he blurted, realizing almost instantly that that was not the question he'd wanted to ask.

"Aside from her performing here every night – excuse me, "appearing nitely," I think is how the flyers go, right?" The bartender paused for a moment. "Well, I guess there might be a few things I could tell," he began. "But really, I think it's probably nothing you couldn't learn from asking her yourself." Robert blinked. The bartender smiled. "You heard correctly. She's here after her set, in the green room. See that door over there, near the stage exit?" He pointed. "We have a little green room for the talent. Ain't much, but then, this is just a local bar." The bartender shrugged. "Should still be back there. Go on, introduce yourself. Ask your questions."

Robert could feel himself start to blush. "Oh, I couldn't," he began, before the bartender interrupted. "Go on, Rob. Really." Still, Robert stood there, as if unable to move. "Go on, live a little, huh?"

Whether it was the repeated urging or something in the bartender's tone, Robert wasn't sure, but he found himself nodding in agreement. "You know, you're right." He squinted towards the stage area and pointed. "That door, right? The red one?" The bartender nodded. "Well then," said Robert, grinning like what he hoped someone at ease looked like, "Wish me luck!" and headed towards the green room before indecision could claim him again.

However, when he arrived at the scarred green door, Robert's previous confidence fled, and he hesitated, indecisive hand hovering instead of knocking. Finally, screwing up his remaining courage, he knocked on the green room door. He waited, but there was no response. Robert knocked once more, louder, but there was still no response.

Shrugging, Robert turned on his heel and headed back towards the bar. Seeing him walking up, the bartender called out, "Not there? May wanna check out in the alley. Might be grabbing a smoke with her manager or the band or something." He pointed to the right. "That far door leads out to the alley. Technically, nobody's supposed to smoke out there, but..." The bartender trailed off. Nodding, Robert veered off towards the door indicated.

He'd placed his hand on the knob when he heard the sound of voices raised, in what sounded like an argument. Robert paused, straining his ears to better determine what was happening before opening the door. The words remained indistinct, though decidedly angry sounding; Robert had just about made up his mind to push open the door when suddenly he heard what sounded like a scream – a scream that was abruptly cut off by a gunshot. Robert could hear someone rushing out of the alley as he flung the door open.

But there was nobody in the alley. Aside from the lingering smell of cordite, some cigarette butts, and what looked like a couple of bloodstains, Robert was alone.

Confused, Robert returned through the door into the bar's main room. He was positive about what he'd heard, and while the alley certainly suggested that something had happened, there was nothing of substance. No shell casings, no body, hell, no proof that those stains were not there beforehand, let alone even blood. And yet, Robert remained sure that something had happened.

He approached the bar, waving his arms to attract the bartender's attention. "Something happened in the alley! Call the police!" said Robert, pointing back to the green room door. "I heard what sounded like an argument, and gunfire. Could be that someone's hurt, or dead even!"

The bartender seemed strangely unconcerned, barely looking up from the drink he was pouring. Robert was taken aback. "Maybe you didn't hear me," he began. "Oh, I heard, Robert, I heard. Stay cool." The bartender finished his pouring out. "Now. What did you see?"

Robert felt his face growing flushed. "Well, I didn't *see* anything," he stammered. "But I heard raised voices, followed by a gunshot and screams. That sounds like something happened!" "Yes, Robert, I agree. But again – did you, in fact, see anything? I know, I know, you heard something. But sounds like you saw nothing, right?" Robert nodded. "I think in order to get the cops into this, we would probably need something more than what you heard." Robert started to protest, but the bartender continued. "I'm not saying nothing happened, or that nothing will be done. If something needs to be handled here, we'll handle it." He pointed to the door. "Go on home, Robert. I'll make sure this gets dealt with. Come back tomorrow night, maybe."

Incredibly, Robert found himself nodding in agreement. He was several blocks into his walk home before it fully clicked that he'd left the club, and the events of the evening. There's no way I sleep, he thought as he made his way into the bedroom. I'll be up all night thinking about this. So saying, he climbed into his bed, the words still on his lips as he blacked out.

The next day found Robert unable to focus on much of anything. Replaying the previous night's sequence of events, he kept trying to figure out what exactly had happened out there. What had he seen, or rather, hadn't? Would it have been any different if he'd arrived sooner, perhaps, or had pushed open the door instead of waiting? These questions and others chased themselves over and over in a loop. Robert contemplated calling the bar, going so far as to punch in half of the number he found on one of their branded matchbooks before stopping. No, he thought. The bartender said to come back, so that's what I'll do. I'll go and see. I will wait until then, and I will go see.

Night finally fell on what felt like the longest day Robert had ever encountered. Searching his closet, he found himself cursing upon discovering that the cleanest things he had were, in fact, the very clothes he'd worn the night before. These will just have to do, Robert thought to himself. I somehow forgot to do laundry and now the day has passed. I doubt anyone will really notice though. Figuring himself dressed sufficiently, he made one final check in the mirror before heading out in search of answers.

Some minutes later, Robert found himself outside From Scratch. As before, a strange nervousness washed over, and he stood there, listening to the bar's neon sign buzzing through the window a minute before putting a hand on the door to open it. Robert sucked in his breath, and walked in, mentally trying to prepare himself for what he would find.

But as he walked towards the bar, Robert felt a weird sense of déjà vu wash over him, that only grew as he went deeper into the bar's darkness. I know I was here only just last night, he thought as he scanned the room. But if I am not mistaken, this looks like the same crowd that was here last night. I mean, I suppose I can get bar regulars, or fans of the music, but they look like they're even wearing the exact same clothes as last night. He looked around for the bartender. Hell, I think that's even the same song on the jukebox.

Robert looked for the bartender but couldn't seem to locate him. Frustrated, he looked for a place to sit, realizing with a slight shock that the only booth open was the same one from last night. This can't be, he thought. It just can't. I know what my eyes are telling me, but this seems too weird. There must be an explanation. Still ruminating in confusion, Robert suddenly became aware of a familiar lull in the bar's noise and dimming of the already low lights. He looked up towards the stage as a single spotlight spiked down, his eyes widening in frightened confusion as Diamond Lil walked out onto the stage.

This cannot be happening, Robert thought in a panic. I know what I heard, what I saw. The gunshot, the blood – it can't be. This cannot be real. But as he sat there, watching Diamond Lil perform a set identical to the previous night's, it became clear that it was.

As with the night before, the songs ended; Diamond Lil sketched her wave and evaporated, leaving Robert to blink in confusion at the empty stage. He rose, momentarily frozen between heading towards the bar to find the bartender, or towards the green room. He told me, "Come back tomorrow night," almost like maybe he knew, thought Robert. At the very least, there's something he's not telling me. Finally unsticking himself, he headed to the bar and what he hoped would be answers.

The bartender had returned to his post by the time Robert made his way through the post-performance crowd. He slid a tumbler of rye across before Robert could even speak, fixing him with a look that was hard to read. Robert could feel his throat closing up. "You knew," he said, the words coming out in a strengthless croak. "You had to."

The bartender looked at Robert for a moment. Picking up a glass and polishing it, he said, easily, "I'm afraid I don't quite follow. Knew what?" He looked at Robert, unblinkingly.

But Robert was undeterred. "You and I both know what I'm talking about." The bartender just stared and kept polishing glasses. "You can act like you have no idea, but I'm not buying it." The bartender still said nothing. Waving his arm at the stage, Robert went on, "The show tonight." "What, something wrong with the performance?" said the bartender. Robert ignored this. "More than the show though? *Her*," he said, with emphasis on the last.

"What's wrong with her?"

"Oh, nothing, I guess. Aside from hearing what sounded like a violent argument that ended in murder, or at, the very least, serious injury." Robert struggled to keep his voice under control. "Nothing wrong there at *all.*" He glared at the bartender.

"So then, what *is* wrong? I mean, you saw her, you saw the show, everything's fine. Nothing doing." Robert said nothing. "Go on, now. What's wrong with that?"

Robert exploded. "What's wrong? What's wrong? EVERYTHING, that's what! I come here last night, you seem to know me. What I drink. For chrissake, even my name, even though I've never been here before."

"I wouldn't be so sure," the bartender murmured.

"And then all that stuff after the show, with the blood and violence. You, practically shoving me out the door, telling me, "Come back tomorrow," which I do."

"So you did."

"Only to witness this!" Robert waved his arms wildly. "This?" said the bartender. "Yes, THIS." Said Robert, practically screaming. "THIS. This, where it's like last night again: I walk in the bar, hear the same song on the jukebox at exactly the same spot, see the exact same people, sit in the exact same spot in the exact same booth that just happens to be open, watch the exact same performance happen the exact same way it did before." He paused. "I'm pretty sure I watched you serve the same drinks in the same order, and polish the glasses the exact same way, too." Robert looked around. "I'm pretty sure that everyone in here is dressed exactly the same as they were last night as well."

He sucked in a huge breath and let it out slowly. "*That* is what's wrong."

There was a brief silence. The bartender finished polishing the glass; he set it down, looked Robert in the eye and said, "And?"

Robert looked at the bartender in amazement. "What do you mean, and? How is this possible?" The bartender merely smiled. "Well? How?"

Putting his polishing rag down, the bartender looked at Robert. "Does it really matter how?" Robert started to protest, but the bartender cut him off. "I mean, think for a moment. Would knowing that make a difference, change anything?" Robert started to speak again, but the bartender continued, as if he hadn't, "I know what you're thinking. I do."

"You're thinking, "I've seen events that I cannot explain. Things for which I have no answer. Things that, if I'd maybe acted differently, could have turned out differently." The bartender picked up another glass. "Except, of course, you couldn't, and even if you could, nothing would have changed." He put the glass down and picked up another. "I think, maybe, somewhere, you know what I'm saying is true. Maybe you don't want to know what you're coming to know, but you do, Robert. You do. Just think for a second."

Robert stood there, thinking. All these things, so exactly the same, as though nothing had happened the night before...even that song...

And then, as he remembered the rest of the words to the song, it hit him. "...Everyone will leave at exactly the same time...When this party's over, it will start again..."

"Will not be any different, will be exactly the same," finished the bartender. "I think maybe now you understand a little bit better?"

"But surely this isn't...I mean...it can't be..." said Robert through lips he could hardly feel.

"Heaven?" said the bartender. "I'm afraid not. But don't look so down."

Author's Note:
I suspect a lot of writers have stuff appearing in dreams. Pretty sure there's a few stories about such incidents (dreams and the weird works that came from them). In this case, this was a dream I kept having about a guy who kept seeing the same thing over and over, down to the same people saying/doing the same thing over, as if no time ever passed. Like they were unaware of anything being off.

I think the original version of this played out differently in my head – dude never really gets what's going on (allegorically speaking) and if remembering right, ends up the murder victim himself.

Far more convoluted and logically problematic (if we're assuming dreams need to have such things like logic.)

I think this variant worked out way better.

10

CLOSE ENCOUNTERS OF A DIFFERENT KIND

Somewhere Outside of Tyler, Texas

It was a good ways before dawn but still late enough that most folks with good intentions and decent jobs were asleep when Earle saw the UFOs. He'd wandered a ways off from the truck where he and Ray-Vern had been drinking away their troubles. Or at least Ray-Vern's troubles; Earle couldn't quite recall; there'd been a fair bit of beer, everything was fuzzy, and he had to piss something fierce. So he'd stumbled away in hopes of a place to pee that didn't have no nettles or fire ants when he saw the lights off them UFOs.

Leastways, he figured they were UFOs even if he didn't see nothin' obvious like anything shaped like a saucer because of the lights. Plane lights didn't do what he just saw, not even in the movies. The way Earle figured, no government would make planes lights that had weird changing colors and patterns, not even someplace known for such foolishness like France so it had to be extraterrestrial. Just had to be. This idea – that visitors from space were not only real but nearby – made it so that even being so full of Lone Star as to have pale yellowish eyes Earle couldn't pee for the excitement, and ran stumbling, with eyes like startled jackrabbits, to find Ray-Vern.

Given the aforementioned Lone Stars and darkness (Texas summer nights being hot enough to make a body think it's two in the afternoon on the sun, but still dark as midnight in a mineshaft) it took Earle some sweaty minutes and a few tries to find the truck. When he finally made it (narrowly missing the passenger mirror and an unpayable dental bill), first words outta Ray-Vern's mouth were, "You know your lil cowpoke's showin', right?" Earle looked down; apparently, in his excitement and haste to report back on the impending alien invasion, he'd forgotten to zip up. He hastily yanked the tab up on his Wranglers; "Man, Ray-Vern, you ain't gonna believe what I just seen!"

"What, other than your dick flopping around like one of them garter snakes been run over by a bicycle?" At this, Earle flushed, face going a deep red that was luckily lost in the dark; "Yeah. Other than that." There was a moment of awkward silence as he pondered, almost audibly, the value in proceeding; he just knew that failure to zip up was gonna cost him somehow.

Finally, Ray-Vern broke the quiet with the subtlety of a fart in church when the preacher's talking about heavenly rewards: "So you gonna tell me or what? You came bustin' over here like your ass was on fire – what's got you all worked up?" The silence held until Earle just couldn't no more – comments and jokes be damned, he just had to spill. "Aliens, Ray-Vern! I mean, like them UFO extraterrestrial things, flyin' around! I seen 'em!"

Ray-Vern was silent a moment, a contemplative look resting easily if somewhat lightly on his face. "UFOs, huh? You seen a UFO? Where?" "Over that ways – up past that hill in between them trees, and over a bit." Earle waved wildly and a trifle unsteadily behind him; "I had to piss something fierce when these crazy lights zoom by, like one not on a plane. I knew they just had to be from space or another dimension or something. A place like that. So then I come find you."

Ray-Vern looked past Earle, towards the area indicated. "Is this like the time you seen a Bigfoot down at the market?"

Earle looked at Ray-Vern, confusion giving way to ire. "Goddammit, Ray-Vern! You wanna call me a liar, call me a liar – I know what I saw!" Ray-Vern pointed off to where Earle had indicated; "Maybe you saw something, but what I see now is a bunch of nothing. No lights, no UFOs, or even any planes, which is likely what you saw but was so drunk you thought it was aliens." He waved outwards in an extravagant gesture, to demonstrate all the nothing, yelling, "Hey! You alien dudes! If you're out there, show yourselves!" before doubling up with laughter.

"You're a real sonofabitch, Ray-Vern. You know that? I mean, when I think of all the shit you sa –" Earle started to say when the lights he'd seen previously reappeared, zooming overhead like a pair of drunken beach balls. This sudden emergence caused Earle to stop mid sentence, leaving whatever shit Ray-Vern said a mystery for the ages. The lights passed overhead, swirling and bouncing before disappearing over the crest of the hill, followed by a colorful haloing, suggestive of a landing of some kind. "Think maybe they heard you, Ray-Vern?"

There appeared on Ray-Vern's face a fleeting look could have been frightened doubt, or at least a cousin close enough to pass, before being snorted derisively away. "I think it's something that we need to look at. But aliens? Little greeeeeeeen (this part drawled out long because he knew it would piss off Earle) men from Mars? I doubt it. Prolly just a plane or a balloon or something."

And with that proclamation, Ray-Vern headed up the hill towards the lights that were still clear and colorful in defiance of any attempt to ignore them. Earle trotted fast on Ray-Vern's heels, trying to shake off the vestiges of residual beeriness.

"Goddammit, Ray-Vern, slow down. Was me who even saw 'em first and here you are, trying to leave me out." Earle sped up, as he could hardly see Ray-Vern in the gloom, "Well, hurry your ass up then. I doubt them moon men or whatever wait forever" floating back.

Earle hauled ass to catch up, almost running into Ray-Vern's back. "Supposing – and I mean, just supposing – this is some alien shit, and there **are** dudes from space there, I reckon we should try to communicate, right? I mean, not like in no movies or anything. Not any dumb shit about taking to meet our leader or whatever, is what I'm saying. But communicate, you know? Talk with 'em."

Ray-Vern remained silent.

"Well, I aim to say something anyhow. Maybe ask 'em something about themselves or where they came from. Natural type questions, show 'em we ain't a threat. People in movies always get so twitchy with UFOs, not really a shock it gets bad so fast." Earle knew he was rambling, but Ray-Vern just kept tramping on, saying nothing. "What you gonna say to 'em, Ray-Vern?" Silence. "Ray-Vern? You gonna ask 'em anything?" Earle strained his ears, trying to hear over the sounds of their boots on the brush underfoot in case he missed something. Finally, he heard it – the low sounds of someone trying to repress laughter. "GOD DAMN YOU RAY-VERN, DON'T YOU GO ASK 'EM IF THEY SEEN MY DICK!" Against this outburst, Ray-Vern could no longer hold back his laughter. He started to say, "Well, ain't like it would be a long discussion or nothin'," but then crested the hill with Earle, causing the words to just fart out like escaping helium from a balloon.

As Ray-Vern and Earle stared, the colors that had both attracted and drawn the two men stopped their light show and were replaced a softer whitish glow. This not only made Ray-Vern and Earle stop feeling like they'd wandered into a Pink Floyd laser show with busted speakers, but served to illuminate and outline what lay at the foot of the hill. Ray-Vern sucked in his breath, and almost immediately wished he hadn't, or at least had him a Tic-Tac, beer and venison jerky breath causing a momentary stomach hitch-up.

Last thing he wanted was to throw up, specially not in front of Earle, because damn it all, he was *right*. There, in the low glowing at the bottom of the slope looked to be a vehicle that hard though he might not want to, Ray-Vern could not NOT call a spaceship.

Goddamn that Earle, thought Ray-Vern. Of all the times for him to be right about something, it's some weird ass shit like this. He thought for a moment on this, eyes never straying from the craft in front of them. Maybe it ain't actually something from space. Could be a rogue special effect, from some movie shit filming around here we don't know about. Or government foolishness. In fact, I bet that's what it is. Government's so stupid, they make fucked up stuff that can't fly for shit with citizen tax-dollars. I'm probably lookin' at a bunch of my money sitting there like a reject from *E.T.* or somethin'.

This idea that Ray-Vern was warming to – that of governmental malfeasance and dumbshittery – was dashed by a whirring sound as the side of the craft irised open, and two seemingly humanoid figures emerged. Shit, shit, SHIT, thought Ray-Vern. They could still be some dumbfuck pilots, but I think it's time to face it that ol' Earle may well be on the mark and these boys are aliens. Ain't this something *indeed*. What are we gonna do now?

Earle thumped Ray-Vern in the back hard enough to make Ray-Vern's teeth click so forcefully that he was glad he wasn't the type to do his heavy thinking with his tongue out like a dog on a Sunday car ride. "Goddamn, Earle – what you tryin' to do, dig for gold with that bony ass elbow?!" "I told you, Ray-Vern, I TOLD you! I knew they was aliens and lookit – there they are!"

Earle was trying his best to both gloat and whisper, resulting in a strangled crowing. "Now, what're we gonna do?" "Why the hell you askin' me," Ray-Vern said under his breath. "You was the one jabbering about what we should ask – where they're from, if they like chunky or smooth peanut butter and all that shit. Now's your chance. Ask 'em something!"

The figures from the ship moved closer to the two transfixed men. Earle stood there, furiously trying to think of what he wanted to ask. "Go on, Richard Dreyfuss – say something to 'em!" Ray-Vern hissed in Earle's ear, nearly causing him to pass out from the halitosis. Earle had had about enough – drinking so-so beer in the dark where you just knew you'd stand in fire ants before the night was up, being ridiculed for anatomy AND belief in the extraterrestrial – it was all more than he could rightly stand for anymore. "Fuck you, Ray-Vern. Don't you be ordering me around, not in front of folks. You ain't the boss of me," and stepped away, moving closer to the visitors.

Once out of the cloud of Ray-Vern's breath (which truly was the sort of shit that should be registered as a deadly weapon), Earle noticed that in addition to not smelling beer, venison jerky, old sweat and leather – the expected smells of themselves – there was an observable absence of the smell of anything. No woodsy smell or lingering dust; no deer shit, no *nothing*. It was almost as if the visitors had surrounded the immediate area with a bubble of scentless clear air. This ability to so subtly yet effortlessly alter the environment spooked Earle a bit in a way he couldn't rightly say. It wasn't threatening – if anything, it was pretty nice – but the idea that they could just do that seemed unnatural. But that was neither here nor there, thought Earle, and here we are. Ain't nothing left to do but keep on. Earle cleared his throat; the moment was now if ever it was gonna be. "Howdy, uh, y'all. Where are you from?"

The figures from the unidentified cra – fuck it, spaceship – moved closer to Earle, close enough for both men to determine that for all of Ray-Vern's wishing, these were indeed some strange-looking dudes not likely from any nearby airbase. They were a little on the short side, about five foot eight, with the one on the left being a tiny bit taller. They were wearing what at first looked like some shiny metallic fabric left over from a failed disco group but upon closer inspection appeared to be a part of them, melding almost perfectly into their pore-less skin.

However, their choice of attire and enviable skin wasn't what made Ray-Vern and Earle feel more certain of an alien origin. It wasn't even the spaceship behind them, quietly burbling like a well-tuned hot rod on TV with the volume down low, though that surely played a part. More than anything else, it was the nagging feeling that even those these dudes had just dropped in out from the night sky like a jet-powered acid trip, Ray-Vern and Earle had seen them before, and knew them somehow. They stared at the visitors, trying to figure out how this was possible. Then it hit them almost simultaneously, the realizations coming with split-second delay like a reverb speaker.

"Son of a bitch, Earle – they look just like that guy on *Mork & Mindy*!" "Robin Williams?" "If I'd meant Robin Williams I'da said Robin Williams, numbnuts. Naw, that other dude, one that played their kid. Jonathan somethin'." "Winters?" "Yeah, him." "Huh, now that you mention it…"

It was true. Both of the ship's inhabitants did bear an uncanny resemblance to the actor, albeit slightly shorter and vaguely bluish. At this point, Ray-Vern and Earle were more than a little sure of these being aliens before them; however, as veterans of more than a few late-night movie marathons between them, they figured it best to proceed with caution, not be too quick and make sure. "As my uncle Farley used to say, if you gonna be bit by a snake, best know what kind of snake." Ray-Vern was fond of this expression and threw it at Earle every chance he got. Earle, who figured it maybe best not to be in many spots as to be snake-bitten as possible, just let that one slide. He looked at Ray-Vern, who kept staring and blinking at the Winters doppelgangers like he had sand in his eye. Earle sighed;

he'd figured it would likely be him doing the talking to the aliens, but it would have been nice if Ray-Vern had at least tried.

"Uh hey guys. I know I ast you before but maybe you're shy a bit, and we startled you. Sorry about that. Me n' Ray-Vern, we ain't gonna hurt you or nothin'. Where y'all from?" A momentary silence fell, as Winters One on the left looked over to Winters Two before speaking. After a few seconds, Winters One replied, slowly in a low voice with a faint metallic buzz, "Texas. We...are Texans." Winters Two nodded his assent. "We are both Texans."

Ray-Vern nudged Earle hard enough to knock his look of surprise to a place where it could get stepped on by a stray boot. "You hear that shit, Earle? You believe that shit? What kinda shit is this?" "Goddamn, Ray-Vern, think you could say shit again, only maybe louder so they hear you?" said Earle from the corner of his mouth. "I mean, yeah that sounds kinda like horseshit to me too, but I don't know. I mean they could be dudes from outer space, which seems likely given everything. Or – just wait a minute – they could be actually from Texas, like from Dallas or Austin or one of those lowlife places where people got money and no taste. They talk all fucked up, too, not like you or me – y'know, regular folks – but like one of those yappy dog breeds that shits too much. They could be some those folks, fuckin around doing whatever weird shit it is people like that do. I still am inclined to think they're aliens myself, but I seen enough movies to risk pissing 'em off unnecessarily. So maybe they're from space, maybe from Richardson. I say we keep going slow until we know."

Ray-Vern, while not one to typically listen to Earle deeply let alone agree, allowed that perhaps he, Earle, was on to something and that caution was advisable. "Texans, huh? Well, that's great! Me n' Ray-Vern here, we're Texans too! Guess y'all just must be from somewheres else further out or something. What are y'all's names?"

Winters Two looked at Winters One, again with an almost imperceptible and undefinable bit of silent communication taking place. Winters Two looked at Earle and said "I am called Billy. He is...Bob." "Billy and Bob is that right?" said Earle. Well then, y'all surely must be Texans, names like that. "Ain't that somethin', Ray-Vern?" He nudged Ray-Vern. "I said, ain't that something?" Ray-Vern, who'd been unable to stop staring, frozen like a statue in a Stetson, came to a bit; "Uh yeah. Yeah! I mean, names like Billy and Bob, they gotta be alright." Saying that, Ray-Vern let his mouth snap shut, letting an uncomfortable silence fall over the night.

This was gonna be one of them long-ass nights, thought Earle. Fuck. Best not let 'em know we know that they ain't named nothin' like Billy and Bob, let alone bein' no Texans. Dallas people may be all fucked up but them two are surely yankin' our dicks if they think we really buy this shit. Still, they seem friendly enough. Friendly or not though, what we can't do is stand around flap jawing all night. Earle looked over at Ray-Vern, who had gone back to staring at Billy and Bob like they were a sign for free beer at the strip club. Worse still was the grin on Ray-Vern's face, all rubbery and as genuine as a politician's promise. He cut eyes back over at the visitors, who while watching them, seemed unaffected by Ray-Vern's antics.

Hot as the night already was, Earle could feel himself start sweating – that trickly back sweat that indicated creeping panic in the face of uncertainty and made you feel like you maybe shit yourself. Earle hated that sensation. Still, nasty back sweat or not, the reality was that he and Ray-Vern seemed to be in a situation that he had no solutions for – at least, none that didn't involve the two of 'em getting shot, probed, or pickled by either Billy and Bob or the feds, none of which sounded like a fair ending to Earle. Unable to shake the visions of specimen jars, and various alien unpleasant things, he opened his mouth, not exactly sure of what to say when a soft blue light washed over him and Ray-Vern, leaving but the faintest afterimage and a strange sense of peace and agreeableness.

The one who called himself Billy now looked at Earle and said, "As much...fun as we are having, could we go somewhere else?" He looked over to Bob, who nodded. "It is late and the...mosquitoes...are plentiful. Could we come...hang around with you?" Something about the way Billy phrased this sat weird with Earle, but he couldn't quite place what it was – anymore than he could bring himself to disagree. He looked over to Ray-Vern, who had thankfully left off with that creepy fake smile. "Uh yeah, sure. That would be great. We got more beer at

Ray-Vern's place. We could go do that, y'all want."

Billy looked over to Bob, who nodded assent. "Well, shit, Earle. Looks like these boys wanna party. "Earle nodded dumbly; something did not seem quite right but damn if he wasn't still feeling all agreeable. "C'mon y'all n' hop in. Hope you don't mind riding in the back." The visitors from another planet (because shit, that was what they were. Even drunk and zapped with alien brain-rays like Earle and Ray-Vern were, they knew. Somewhere deep down under the beer and mental scrambling they knew, even if words couldn't be found.) hopped in the back of Ray-Vern's truck and away they went into the night. As he watched the dust clouds in the rearview, Earle couldn't shake the feeling that as weird as shit was right at this moment, it was only just beginning.

Earle woke the next morning to find himself on Ray-Vern's couch, with little recollection of the night before, and sunlight hitting him in the face like a landlord kicking down the door on eviction day. Judging from how his head felt (like an inept plumber, high on ideas and low on actual skill, had mistaken his skull for a toilet), Earle figured he and Ray-Vern had been drinking all night, probably somewhere out in bumfuck like usual. They'd done...no...they'd seen...something, though what Earle could not recall. He kept probing at what that something could be, like an aching tooth, but to no avail. Speaking of aches, Earle's head hurt so bad, he figured he'd need to be a set of conjoined twins who lost a bar fight for it to feel worse. Goddamn, thought Earle; just what **did** me and Ray-Vern drink last night? He opened his mouth to yell for Ray-Vern, thought better of it, and was floundering off the couch when Billy walked in.

"Hi, friend Earle. It appears that you may be distressed. Do not be overly alarmed," said Billy, his lightly cyanotic face twisting into a smile that even Jonathan Winters, master of disarming grins, could not have managed. "Everything is fine, and we can explain to you like we have explained already to friend Ray-Vern." Earle stopped his floundering and instead slid back further onto the couch, eyes widening in shock and the memory of last night returning. "I see that you are recalling some of the previous evening but are perhaps still confused. Again, do not be alarmed. We can explain."

Earle remained where he was on the couch, as Billy, still grinning in a way that the real Jonathan Winters would have cried in envy over, was joined by Bob. They both stood a few feet to the left of Earle, blocking the worst of the incoming sunlight, a fact for which Earle was not wholly ungrateful for. Way he saw it, this could still all end up with organs being harvested or at least, the kind of touching you don't want, but these fellas weren't rude. Downright thoughtful, even, like they'd probably apologize for doing something nasty to you before doing it. Earle eased back on to the couch a bit, figuring he could likely still bolt up and away if needed, assuming they didn't use mind control or blasters or whatever it is aliens did to keep ungrateful people from leaving. He looked over at Billy; "Okay, then. Explain."

"Last night, or rather, this morning, you invited us over to...how did friend Ray-Vern state it...party like a motherfucker. This seemed both improbable and intriguing to us, in addition to being very hospitable. So, we came along with you to your domicile. During the course of the revelries, the two of you consumed much of a low-grade intoxicant in liquid form, which seemed to induce you to speak more freely and reveal that you had determined our extraterrestrial origins. This was mildly alarming, as we had not planned on revelation at such a juncture; in turn, we had to render you unconscious so we could discuss our next steps. This accounts for the gaps in your recall function and cranial pain, for which we apologize."

This information, in conjunction with the beer and significant increase in polysyllables, proved to be more than Earle could put together easily; he squinted at Billy and Bob, trying to figure out what he was being told. "Say that again...?" Billy smiled at Earle, and said, not unkindly, "We, as you might say, "knocked you the fuck out" so we could talk and "get our shit together." Hearing these phrases delivered in such flat and serious tones caused Earle to giggle; quickly he got control of himself. This ain't no laughing matter, dipshit, Earle told himself angrily; these dudes may still wanna cut us up or do butt stuff. Can the laughter and see if they'll tell.

Warily, Earle sat on the couch, watching Billy and Bob while wearing the kind of expression he figured Steve McQueen would have – cool and watchful but not overly suspicious. To Ray-Vern, who had just walked in from the back room, it looked like Earle had maybe bitten his tongue or was trying hard not to fart. "Hey Earle," he said, "what's goin –" "These fellas were just about explain a decision they made that concerns us, Ray-Vern," said Earle. "I figure it might be important so maybe we both should hear this."

"Oh, you mean how you were right that they was from space but not planet X or whatever like you was going on about last night? They're here to observe and make some notes and stuff. Bob there is supposed to do some drawings too, I think." Earle looked at Ray-Vern, dumbfounded. "Yeah, they kinda told me earlier when you was still passed out."

With this, Ray-Vern trailed off, and an awkward silence descended as the four sat there, Earle glaring at Ray-Vern. Finally, Earle could take it no more; he looked at Billy and said, "Ok, I get that everyone (emphasis on every, with a dark look at Bob and Ray-Vern) knows everything and is all hunky-dory and shit, but...but.... what about y'all's spaceship? You want to observe, fine great, but you cain't leave no space vehicle in a field where just anyone could find it. That kinda shit gets attention on you fast, like, well...just fast." Earle trailed off, unsure where to go with this but feeling like he'd raised a valid point that these smartass aliens might have forgotten when they was busy telling Ray-Vern stuff.

Billy smiled indulgently at Earle – the way you would at a sweet but not always bright dog that can't quite break the habit of eating its own poop – and said, "Not to fear, friend Earle. We have taken the necessary precautions. We have, you might say, got this handled." Earle looked at Billy and Bob, unconvinced. "Please observe," said Billy, moving away from the window and pointing. Earle squinted through the grime on Ray-Vern's living room window to see what looked like a battered red 1978 Trans Am sitting in the driveway on cinder blocks. For a moment it didn't register; when it finally did, Earle let out a whistle. "Say...that's pretty clever!"

"It was really Bob's idea," said Billy. At this, Bob beamed; "He's the creative one." Earle looked over at Ray-Vern, who was very conspicuously not looking at him. Maybe these aliens were indeed on the level, he thought. Maybe they DO just wanna observe. Still, something nagged at him. "Well...okay. Seems like y'all are serious enough. And maybe y'all just wanna observe us. But one thing I don't get is why us," said Earle, a plaintive note creeping in. "We ain't exactly nobody special, like scientists or military or anything slightly famous. Hell, Ray-Vern ain't even got a job." At this last, Ray-Vern's head jerked around, a dark flush coloring his neck. "Of all the people in the whole state, why us?" Earle noticed that during this last part, he'd stood up and now, having been so plainly revealing, felt exposed. He sat back down, unsure of where to go from there.

Billy started to say something but was interrupted by Bob. "What you say is, however unintentionally self-degrading, is true, friend Earle. However, despite that, and irrespective of other criteria which we will not elaborate upon, it was your unforced pleasant and hospitable disposition that ultimately influenced our decision." Earle stared at Bob, uncomprehendingly. "He means they chose us cuz we was nice to 'em, dumbass," whispered Ray-Vern into Earle's ear. "Yes, precisely. Your kindness suggested cooperation and a greater likelihood of success," Bob continued, moving closer to Earle, still seated on the couch. "As stated previously, I sincerely...we sincerely apologize for any distress caused by the prior subterfuge and hope this all makes amends. We will observe for a short period of time and then depart, with no one but you two the more knowledgeable."

Earle looked over at Ray-Vern, who looked like he was going to say something that was most likely another explanation but then thought better of it. He thought about this for a minute. "This all sounds good and whatnot, but I guess before we all shake hands and stuff, I gotta ask – why all this dancing around? Seems like y'all could have just made us do what you wanted, whether we wanted to or not." To this, both Bob and Billy nodded their assent. "This is indeed true, friend Earle – we could have indeed compelled you more forcibly," said Bob, "but this would not have produced the desired data. That, and as noted – you were kind to us. It would have been unseemly to compel compliance more forcefully."

Earle allowed how this was pretty true and that it was hardly sporting to use mind control or whatever it was they did to manipulate him or Ray-Vern into helping them – specially when they'd been nice enough to invite 'em to hang out. "Well, I guess it's all okay. I mean, seems like y'all mean what you say about observing and things. Given you coulda just mind-controlled us or zapped us into dust or whatever but didn't." A look of dismay crossed both Billy and Bob's faces; Jonathan Winters frowning in stereo. Earle ignored this. "So, it's cool. Y'all can hang out here and do your observing or whatever else it you came for." He paused for a minute. "I do got one more question, though."

"What's that, friend Earle?" said Billy. "Have we not answered and clarified to your satisfaction?" "Oh no, nothing like that," said Earle hastily. "I was just wondering – I gathered y'all dudes got some pretty sophus...er...fistic...uhh...some fancy tech that allows you to change the way things look, like that car out there that's really y'all's ship, or that y'all both look like Jonathan Winters. But uhh...why Jonathan Winters?" Billy looked at Bob, who looked over at Ray-Vern. "It was something we got from him," said Bob, pointing at Ray-Vern. "Apparently there was some sort of visual programming in the past that friend Ray-Vern was fond of that involved beings from space. We picked this up in our initial scan of you and figured that would make for a suitable enough and non-threatening appearance."

Earle looked over at Ray-Vern, who shrugged. *"Mork and Mindy*, huh?" Ray-Vern shrugged again. "Guess we should just be glad it wasn't *ALF*, or worse, that fuckin' *Space Precinct*."

The next few weeks passed in a blurry haze. True to their word, Billy and Bob observed, made drawings, and only looked like Jonathan Winters when hanging with Ray-Vern and Earle, so as not to raise any suspicions in the town. Everything seemed unchanged, aside from the occasional neighbor asking about "Ray-Vern's sweet new ride" and wondering when it would be finished. Still, something felt off to Earle. He couldn't put a finger on it, but there was something different about the town. It wasn't exactly a sinister feeling, or foreboding, but still, it nagged at Earle, forever at the edge of his periphery. This feeling followed him like a stray animal demanding attention yet determined to remain out of reach, until the evening he noticed on his way over to Ray-Vern's that there were wheels on the Trans-Am.

Earle burst into Ray-Vern's, yelling for him to come look. "Lookit that, Ray-Vern

– see them wheels? I think those two are about to leave." Ray-Vern looked at Earle. "So? Dunno why you seem upset, way you been going on about things feeling off. I'd think this might set your mind at ease or something." "That ain't the point, Ray-Vern – I mean, yeah I guess maybe that got something to do with it but it still don't seem right, them just getting up and leaving like they ain't gonna say nothing, just go." Earle threw himself on the couch and stared at the front door, as if willing Billy and Bob to appear. They sat there on the couch, Ray-Vern idly thumbing through a car magazine and Earle glaring at the door until they noticed an aroma drifting in from out back. "Say, Ray-Vern...you smell something?" "Yeah, come to think of it...smells a lot like brisket."

Earle yanked the door to the backyard open, to see what the source of the delicious smell was, only to find Billy and Bob behind Ray-Vern's ancient and under-utilized smoker. He yelled back, "Goddammit, Ray-Vern! You mean to tell me them two been here the whole time I was staring at the front door like a lovesick hound dog with a dead master?!" "Calm down, Earle – ain't like I knew they was out here. I was takin' a nap when you showed up, rippin' down the door like a wild hog with a load of shot in his ass, yappin' about tires and leaving and shit." "Well shit, Ray-Vern..."

This commotion drew the attention of the alien duo, who moved away from the smoker, hurrying towards Earle and Ray-Vern bickering near the steps leading down into the backyard. "Friend Earle, friend Ray-Vern, what seems to be the concern?" said Billy, armed with a meat fork and a frown. "You appear upset." "I seen them tires on the Trans-Am," accused Earle. "That means y'all are done observing and was just gonna drive off until you could change back into a spaceship and leave without sayin' nothin' and that ain't right. After how nice we been, it seems mighty unkind just to wanna take off like that." He backed away from Billy and Bob, unaware that his lower lip was quivering a little.

"Friend Earle, I think you have this all wrong and are upset over nothing. Yes, we are preparing to leave. You are absolutely correct in your surmising that. However, we would never think about simply leaving without a proper farewell." said Billy. "Yes," said Bob. "While it is true that our observational mission is complete and that the stellar alignments are optimal for departure this evening, Billy is correct.

We would never abuse your kindness and hospitality by an abrupt leave-taking. We have been preparing this feast of various burnt flesh for your consumption and enjoyment as a way of demonstration of gratitude."

There was a moment of silence as Bob's polysyllables registered. "You mean, you made us a mess of barbecue to say thanks for crashing here while y'all did your mission?" said Earle. Billy and Bob nodded. "Well shoot, fellas...that's mighty white of you." Billy and Bob shared a look of confusion; "I fail to see what coloration or pigmentation has to do with this preparation, friend Earle," said Bob. "Can you explain?"

"Never you mind, guys. It's just a way of sayin' that was right nice of you." At this, the aliens beamed, pleased. "Thank you, friend Earle. We appreciate the recognition of this. Please, ingest, as we must leave soon, and would like to make the proper leave," said Billy. "Man, it all looks so good, I hardly know where to start," said Earle. "I'm gonna start with that brisket there," said Ray-Vern. "Looks a tad dark, and I ain't seen brisket like that before but damn if it don't smell perfect!"

And with that, both Earle and Ray-Vern dug in. For a full hour a total silence descended upon the yard, punctuated only by the sounds of eating and the occasional belch until Ray-Vern, followed by Earle, put their plates down, groaning. "By god y'all, I think that may have been some of the best barbecue made, as well as the best I ever ate," said Earle. "Y'all might just have to come visit again just so we can get more of that." Ray-Vern nodded his assent, albeit slowly, on account of being overly stuffed. "When y'all planning on heading out?"

"Friend Earle, we will be leaving tonight, around the time we first arrived originally, as that is when the optimal stellar conjunction will be occurring. If you would like to say goodbye at that time, we can accommodate. We will bring you along at the proper time, if you are amenable to this," said Billy. "We'd like to, if y'all don't mind," said Earle. "Yeah, that would be right nice," said Ray-Vern. "But if y'all don't mind, I think I might need a nap first, as I seem to have eaten a bit too much." And with that, he turned around and went into the house, Earle trailing behind, headed for the couch.

Earle awoke from a dream in which he'd been being chased by a giant anthropomorphic taco, to Billy and Bob gently shaking him. As the taco had been wielding a knife and screaming something about the need for extra salsa, Earle welcomed the interruption. "Whazz goin' on, fellas? Is it time?" he asked. "Yes, friend Earle. It is time we departed. However, we could not wake Ray-Vern. Perhaps you could assist?" said Bob.

"Why, sure, I'd be delighted," said Earle, a mischievous grin slowly spreading across his face. "He's kinda hard of hearing when he's dead ass like that. Let me show y'all what needs doin'." They all wandered into Ray-Vern's bedroom. "Now, when I raise my hand like this," gesturing with his left hand, "I want everyone to yell, real loud like, "WAKE UP, ASSHOLE!" said Earle. "That should do the trick nicely." Billy and Bob looked skeptical but readied themselves. Earle raised his hand, all three yelling in unison; Ray-Vern jerked awake as though electro-shocked, letting loose a massive fart in the process. He glared at Earle who smiled sweetly and said, "That was for all them dick jokes," before following the aliens out to the car.

Now thoroughly awake, the four of them – Billy, Bob, Earle and an annoyed Ray-Vern piled into the Trans-Am that, for a disguised spaceship, looked amazingly like a Trans-Am on the inside as well, down to the aging Joe Walsh 8-track in the player and the overflowing ashtray. As they drove out, headed to the piney scrub outside of town, Earle was only just able to remind himself that this was indeed a spaceship, as nothing that ever rolled off that California assembly line ever handled that smooth. As the wheels turned, and the road disappeared, he tried to think of something to say to fill the silence. Usually, when driving out this way, Ray-Vern had the radio blaring, to a point where conversation was nigh well useless.

Somehow, Earle didn't think music was appropriate here, assuming he could find something all of them liked. He and Ray-Vern listened to country mostly, mostly because Ray-Vern liked it, and it was usually Ray-Vern's truck they were in. Earle himself liked a mix of things but figured it was not worth the sweat and jawing mentioning that would bring. No, music was out. As the car continued out further into the night, Earle wracked his brain for something to say, if for no other reason than to fill the silence and perhaps quiet that nagging feeling that had crept back in during the ride. He'd run through the standard small talk gambits – inquiries about having had a pleasant time, what it would be like back home – and figured these as too late and trivial to mess with. Earle was still working out something to say when he noticed them slowing to a stop.

"Friends Earle and Ray-Vern, we have arrived at the location where we originally met. As we must return our vehicle to its ordinary form, we must ask you to get out." Dutifully, Ray-Vern and Earle slid out from the back seat, moving a few yards from the car upon exit and standing there, the dust from the arrival skirling around their feet. Billy nodded to Bob, who tapped at his wristwatch; this caused the Trans-Am to shimmer and silently change back into its original spaceship form, lights on flickering and twinkling. The aliens turned towards Earle and Ray-Vern, waiting uncertainly.

"As much as we would like to say something profound, we find ourselves unable to convey the words adequate to express accurately. So rather than lessen the moment, we shall depart, mission happily concluded. We thank you, friends Earle and Ray-Vern." And with that, Billy and Bob (or whatever they were called) stepped inside their craft; lights bounced and twirled, and as though it were a fever dream brought on by the flu or some bad chili, the ship was gone.

For some minutes after, they stood there, either unable or unwilling to move. Finally, Earle broke the silence. "You reckon we'll ever see 'em again, Ray-Vern?" Ray-Vern said nothing, just shrugged. "I mean, I dunno. Seems like they might." Again, only a shrug from Ray-Vern. "I mean, I just dunno. While they was real nice and all, I ain't so sure that this is the last, or that they told us everything."

This last elicited more from Ray-Vern, who said, "How do you figure? Seemed to me they was pretty much on the level." "Well, see that's just it, Ray-Vern. It seems like it's all good but I tell you it ain't. Like little things at the back of your mind like you cain't see or figure at first but you know something is up." To this Ray-Vern said nothing, just stared. Earle continued, "Like they was all "we will only observe" like they ain't changing things but they did."

"Changing things? Like what?" asked Ray-Vern.

"You notice how that dog we used to hear every morning,"

"Humper. He was old man Jenkins' dog," interrupted Ray-Vern.

"one that was always in the trash makin' noise stopped," continues Earle. "Like he was just gone?"

"Earle," Ray-Vern said gently, "he was just a dog. Ain't much suspicious about no missin' dog." "Well, what about ol' Ms. Tippins at the end of the block? You know, that lady with them hooters so big probably kicks 'em when she walks that's got the hots for you? Always whistlin' and shit whenever we drive past." Ray-Vern looked at Earle and said, "And? What about her?" "Ray-Vern, she ain't been around neither. Just like Jenkins' dog. Or the postman. Or that snotty-ass kid at the convenience who always talks shit to us. All of 'em, gone."

"So?" said Ray-Vern. "What do you mean, so? I mean, ain't you the least bit concerned here that maybe just maybe them two wasn't playing it straight after all? Like, here's all this mysterious shit that don't add up; for all you know that Bob didn't do no drawings but instead they scoped things out, figuring out how to come back to invade and here you stand, unconcerned like shit is fine, cuz they made us barbecue! For all we know, that barbecue was all them missing people! We could be like beef jerky to them dudes from wherever."

"Well..." said Ray-Vern. "Well, WHAT," said Earle.

"Well," said Ray-Vern. "It WAS really good barbecue," and fell silent.

Author's Note:
A fair number of creative types (or at least, the ones I know) have fairly odd dreams.

Coincidentally, I have a goodish number of folks I know that believe in UFOs/aliens/extraterrestrials. Now, I'm not saying that I don't, mind you –

that would be terrible science – but unlike these aforementioned contemporaries, I do not think they've visited here. Because, you know, space.

It's really big, y'all.

That being said, I had this weird dream about what might happen if we did have some visitors from parts far outside...and the only folks to bear witness are a couple of well...the guys in the story. The dream was, if I recall rightly, most centered initially around the idea of aliens liking barbecue.

It just kinda went out from there.

11

Harmadillos III

Harmadillos Leave Home

Wil Bradford lived in one of the most beautiful enclaves in Austin, Texas, right where Barton Springs turns into Rollingwood Drive. Barely a step from downtown and tucked just west of Zilker Park, his property included a wooded yard that covered an entire quarter acre. Nestled within that yard was an outbuilding with floor-to-ceiling windows that straddled a small ravine. Wil jokingly referred to this as "The Outhouse" because, as he would explain, it was "where he came up with all manner of shit."

Wil spent a good deal of time in The Outhouse, indulging in his painting and ceramics hobbies mostly. But not always. Not every minute within its walls was necessarily craft time. Sometimes, he'd just sit. Sit, and watch the wildlife that would grace his yard with visits from the window in the Outhouse.

Wil loved the urban wildlife at his home, which included a pair of kit foxes, a family of raccoons, and various possums, skunks, and such. In the evenings, he'd cook them spaghetti, which he'd then mix with Gravy Train, leaving it on the cedar deck in the old tin bowl that had belonged to his childhood dog Gracie. The following morning, he'd rinse the bowl, put out fresh suet for the hawks, and hand-feed the fawns that liked to come to his door. Evening ritual, followed by morning ritual – these routines helped give some structure and peace to Wil's life. It was living a dream – a beautiful house on gorgeous land, replete with wildlife friends – or would have been, if not for the extreme anxiety and depression that he'd struggled with since childhood.

When Wil was six, his older brother Charlie died rather unexpectedly. Unable to cope with this loss, their dad had gone out to the barn, tacking up a note – short of words but long in its grief – before putting a shotgun to his mouth. Their mother, who was left to handle the messy aftermath, never quite recovered, dying eleven years to the day from cancer.

Wil, who was 17 at the time, thought that it was something else, no matter what that death certificate said. He knew it was her broken heart, finally unable to cope with the years and the losses.

With both parents now gone, the once beautiful family farm deteriorated, slowly decaying into a southwestern Grey Gardens, unable to serve either man or beast. Wil finished high school in the wake of his mother's death, trying his best to keep up with the farm work, before ultimately submitting to forces more powerful and beyond his control. He auctioned the last head of cattle and listed the farm, buildings, and lands for sale.

The pandemic hit. Some adapted to the emerging work-from-home dynamic and sought affordable housing and expansive space in places outside the city. Wil, struggling with pangs of isolation in the wake of family tragedy, saw this as an opportunity to head into town and start afresh. The farm, which he'd listed for sale and much of which had become a wilderness, sold with a speed that surprised Wil almost as much as the money he realized from it. He rented a condo in the 360 Tower, before realizing after nearly a year, that he missed and needed the rural world almost as much as he needed the buzz of the city. With its location in the city and spacious grounds, his Rollingwood oasis offered the best of everything, allowing Wil to dare hope that he could maybe lay rest to the past, and breathe again.

It was Monday afternoon again; Wil slouched down against the lightly worn channel back sofa, idly thumbing through a dog-eared copy of last June's Highlights for Children as he waited. He contemplated trying the puzzle on the back when he heard the door creak and the clickety-clack of heels down the hall. Sighing, Wil gently tossed the magazine back on the table before standing up and smoothing his shirt.

"Wil, you're welcome to come back. Would you like some water?"

"No, thanks."

Dr. Frankie Watson had a laid-back demeanor and Wil genuinely enjoyed seeing her, even if he, by his own admission, put little stake in talk therapy. His lack of belief in such things notwithstanding, he appreciated her focus on mindfulness and genuine kindness. She was helping him develop coping strategies to get through rougher moments, which was something that Wil did believe in, and valued. The way he saw it, the moments of talk therapy were but a small price to pay.

Wil sat down, bringing his knees together and leaning forward. "The breathing helps," he sighed. "It really does." Wil paused a moment before continuing. "On Redbud, on the way home last night, I thought I saw an armadillo. I pulled over."

Doctor Watson scooted forward slightly. "Go on. Tell me what happened."

"It was hit," Wil continued. "Thought I'd move it out of the road, so it wouldn't get hit anymore, you know? Like I could help, maybe. It was a possum, though, and she was gone." He paused. "I did the breathing thing like we discussed, using that app you told me about. I sat for about five minutes. It helped."

"Thank you for sharing that with me, Wil. I'm glad to hear that. Clearly, you are still processing your unresolved trauma with Charlie's death. You have repressed a lot from that night, as we have touched on in previous sessions. The thing to always remember here, Wil, is that armadillos are gentle creatures." Dr. Watson smiled. "You know, like you. They mostly just want to be left alone. The ones around here aren't going to hurt you. Only maybe next time, you should leave the roadkill to the vultures?" She let out a soft chuckle. "In all seriousness though, I'm proud of you, Wil. This is good progress." She paused. "Do you maybe feel more like trying some of the journaling exercises we discussed?"

Wil groaned internally. He hated journaling; it was the part of therapy he found patronizing, with its cryptic jargon and linguistic flatness. He tried a different tack, to hide his irritation because Doctor Watson was very kind and had been a great help, but it was hard. He really, really hated journaling.

"Perhaps," Wil said, "you can help me find more tactical approaches. The breathing helped. It really did. But...dwelling on the subject...I don't see how that helps. If anything, it just helps me get stuck."

"Emotional processing, Wil. Not dwelling. Dwelling suggests unhelpful circular motions; this is about deliberate and linear forward movement. You'll never be able to overcome your fears if you are unwilling – Wil-ing haha, sorry... if you are unwilling to face your trauma. In vivo or imaginal exposure therapy works well to lessen chronic phobias like yours. We'll work together on this. I think that repeated exposure, combined with relaxation or meditative therapies will help you both examine and restore your relationship with armadillos to a more normative and stable footing. Help me help you. Let's try the journaling, okay?"

"Uhm," Here, Wil fumbled before finally giving up. He knew when he was licked. "Okay. I'll... try it."

Dr. Watson smiled, then frowned. "Oh, Wil, I'm sorry – that's our hour. Great work this week. Keep it up!"

Wil went home. As a package was due, he stopped at the mailbox and was reaching inside when he heard some rustling in the leaves just out of sight, beyond the corner of the house. Remembering his exercises, he inhaled deeply and whispered, "They're gentle like me. They're just little creatures and can't hurt me. They're gentle like me." He repeated this several times before walking inside and tossed the mail – no package, just junk and circulars – on the console by the door.

Wil glanced out the kitchen window; there on the patio were two little armadillos, rooting around in the leaves that had piled up. His breath quickened as he whispered, "Gentle like me. They're just little creatures. Gentle like me." He closed his eyes, trying not to think of Charlie. "They're gentle like me," he breathed, gripping the edge of the counter. Wil watched them roll and rustle in the leaves for a moment, nuzzling in the fresh compost for bugs. I guess they are cute little things, he thought. Like a pillbug and a possum had babies.

Finally able to tear himself away from the window, Wil retired to the TV room, watching reruns of Star Trek until he eventually fell asleep on the sofa. The next morning found him with a stiff neck, the residue of vivid and startling dreams clinging, though just out of the reach of easy recall. He went on with his usual morning routine and, per Doctor Watson's request, spent some time journaling.

The following Monday came and went similarly enough to last Monday that they could have been mistaken for twins in a bad light. Like last week, Wil went to see Dr. Watson. And like last week, the session ended with Doctor Watson's praise. As he was leaving, she challenged him to engage in some "radical self-care" that evening, to "get outside of his normal comfort zone." Despite her usage of the jargon that he despised, the idea did hold some appeal to Wil. He mulled this over on the drive home before deciding that maybe the weather was nice enough for some company and steaks out on the grill.

Once home, Wil fired up the grill and brought his Bluetooth speaker out to the patio. He'd found a great deal on some organic grass-fed beef at the Sprouts near his house (though not as good as the beef his family had raised, he thought with some small satisfaction. Not possible.) and his friend Josh, from high school, would be by in a bit with some beer. They'd grill the steaks and eat them out on the patio and talk. Heading back outside with steaks in hand, Wil smiled; jargon or not, the good doctor was right. This was exactly what was needed, he thought. I'll have to tell her at the session. He was midway through thinking up a witty way to thank Dr. Watson when a noise broke through, shattering his reverie.

Wil froze in place. I know that noise, he thought, mind starting to cycle up into a panic spiral. I *know* that noise. But it can't be. It can't.

The noise – a low, sibilant chittering – sounded again.

Wil squeezed his eyes shut, barely registering that he'd dropped the plate holding the steaks, or the sound made when the plate broke against the patio tiles. This cannot be happening, he thought. There's no way.

I'll just…keep my eyes closed and breathe. When I open them, there will be nothing there that can hurt me. I will breathe and be okay. Wil began inhaling slowly, eyes still closed. Slowly, he let his breath out, repeating the cycle for a full minute before opening his eyes.

But the patio remained steadfastly, stubbornly occupied. From the tiles nearest his Big Green Egg grill, a familiar face regarded him with glowing red eyes.

Wil felt the hair on his head stand on end. This simply cannot be happening, his mind argued. That was years ago, and miles away. This cannot be real. You're just...punishing yourself for wanting to enjoy your life. For Charlie. This is not real. You know it can't be. Say it out loud and it will all go away.

But the words remained locked in his throat.

As the creature moved away from the grill, Wil felt a weird doubling sensation, like time out of joint as the tiles under his feet were momentarily replaced by Hill Country farmland before reappearing. "Run, Wil," whispered Charlie's voice in his head. "You been here before, and you know what happens if you don't. Run."

"Sorry, big brother," thought Wil. "I been running this whole time, and well, look where it's gotten me. I can't. At some point you just got to stand."

Wil looked at the creature approaching. "You know what? I don't believe you're really here. And even if you are, you're just a regular old armadillo. And armadillos are gentle, like me." The creature never paused, but kept slowly advancing, its gaze never wavering. "Gentle, like me."

"Gentle, like me."

Wil was midway through the fourth repetition when the armadillo (or whatever it really was) sprang at him, tearing into his throat, "like me," escaping in a windy rush as he fell, shattering his skull against the patio tiles.

Some time later, Josh arrived. Carrying a twelve-pack of Shiner, he made his way through the house to the patio, calling out to his friend that he was here, and that he was sorry to be late. "Didn't mean to take so long, Wil, but traffic on Mo-Pac was –," the word *killer* drying up in his throat as Josh's brain tried to register what his eyes were telling him.

Wil's patio looked as though a small cyclone had ripped through a paint store, splashing red paint everywhere. The deck chairs were slashed and overturned, with Gracie's old bowl buried under the one that Wil favored. The Big Green

Egg still stood, coals still hot, with two burnt lumps still stuck to the center of the grill. A Bluetooth speaker, scratched and covered in the mess but otherwise no worse for wear, blinked a lonely blue light, as if searching for something it knew it would never find.

Of Wil, there was no further sign.

12

CAKE AND GRAVY

"Well, it's your choice, really..." Burns said lazily, and let the sentence trail off, the silence underscoring how much choice they both knew Murph really had. "But I'm tellin' ya, it's a piece of cake. Easy stuff, simple."

"If it's such a piece of cake, then why ain't you takin' it?" Murph asked.

"Well, I could you know...I really could," said Burns. "Would be no thing at all. But then, I ain't the one hurting for cash. I ain't the one who loused up his last two jobs. I ain't the one in hock up to my eyeballs. I ain't the one who owes the Big O thirty large –"

"That's enough!" said Murph, sharply. But Burns hammered on, all signs of laziness gone – "...I ain't the one who got all tangled up with some skag bag he picked up on the last job. I ain't the one everybody thinks got no stomach left for the biz and gone all soft –"

"I said, that's enough!" said Murph, not quite yelling. Silence at the other end of the phone and then a low chuckle. "What I been trying to say here, Murph. I ain't need to take this one because I ain't you. That's why."

"Piece of cake, really. Nothing to it. You could do it, easy – practically in your sleep," Burns' voice a slow trickle of smoke and honey on the phone. "You're making too much fuss over nothing, Murph. A gravy job. A cakewalk. Really. Nothing to it." A pause, then more smoke and honey, broken by Burns' chuckling, slid through the receiver into Murph's cramped kitchen. "I don't get why you so tense, Murph. You wasn't always that way."

Murph – six foot nothing in socks – jerked his head away from the receiver and glared at it, knuckles whitening in a stranglehold, before sullenly putting it back to his ear. "Wasn't always what way, Burns? Whattya tryna say, huh? Maybe I am, maybe I'm not – what's it to ya, anyway? Maybe I just don't like no calls like this in the morning, huh? Maybe I –"

"Okay, okay, okay – just cool out, huh? Maybe I said something unkosher. Didn't mean to get ya all bent up over it or nothin'. Fine – you the same, I'm the same, everybody's the damn same. Same as it ever was. No need to be gettin' all sore now. Just keep cool, awright?" Burns' voice held a note of anxious sincerity just longer than a blink before oozing more smoke and honey. "Like I said, it's a cake job, a gravy job, fuckin' kids' stuff. Just tryna do ya solid and get you squared some cuz you and me, we go back a ways."

Feathers temporarily smoothed over, Murph lapsed into silence and felt around on the table behind him with one hand for the cigarettes he knew were there. Hooking one foot around the leg of the chair nearest to the phone, he dragged closer and sat down. Murph lit up a cigarette and said in an exhalation of smoke, "Okay, fine then." He fumbled around behind him, again without looking, for the ugly fish-shaped souvenir ashtray he kept on the table. "About this cake. This gravy job that's got you so hopped up. Hit me."

A long silence – long enough for Murph to think that maybe Burns had changed his mind and hung up – when Burns asked, "Ever been to, know of or even *heard* of, a little nothing burg called Nolanville?"

Fishing for another smoke, Murph allowed that he'd heard of it, though not sure when or how. Some stupid bumfuck nowheresville, about an hour away. A real zero – not much more than a church and a couple of crummy houses, with no Dairy Queen and barely a highway sign to announce its existence. "Yeah, that's the place, awright. Figured you might know it. What you probably *don't* know though is that there's a fortune in that little nothing." At this last part, Murph choked and let out a series of harsh caws – a Murph laugh. "Okay, now I *know* this is a joke. Make with the punchline, wouldja?"

"Cuz, see, I been through there before, and there ain't no way there's a fortune in that place. They don't even have no police force or fire department, they so tiny. I bet even God forgot that place exists. So yeah – make with the joke awready, okay?" Murph snorted. "A fortune? In Nolanville? That's either a pipe dream or some kinda yuk. Nolanville." He cawed again.

"You don't hear me laughin', do ya, Murph? That's right, you ain't hearin' none cuz it ain't a joke. Straight goods. If I'm lyin', I'm dyin'. I swear it." The earnest tone of Burns' voice failed to persuade Murph. "Well, guess you better have your last will made up then, because this sounds hinky. We both know this ain't no restaurant, so I dunno why you wanna feed me soup – but that's what this is. Soup. Watery garbage. I don't trust this." Here he paused.

"But you keep tellin' me you ain't jokin' –"

"I'm not." Still smoke and honey, but now with a hint of ice.

"Okay then. You ain't jokin'. And if you ain't jokin', spill it."

"You gonna listen to what I got, and let me frame this out all nice and proper like, or you gonna keep on with what we both already know, all this tough and tired rebop? I don't gotta talk, ya know. Say the word and we can dust this now."

Murph thought for a minute. "Go on. I guess I should hear, seein' as you made the time to call. Sorry I cut onya like that."

Burns continued, making no mention of Murph's apology. "As I was sayin', before that geography lesson – yeah, Nolanville is a nothing. A nowhere. But it's also the same nowhere nothing that Jake Magruder disappeared to, last year, after the McGinley job." Burns paused. "Think back on that job and let that soak in a minute."

Sitting in his kitchen, Murph felt his throat close up, with neither words nor smoke able to escape. Jake "Iceman" Magruder was the stuff of bigtime heist legends. Ten years ago, Magruder hit the First National in McGinley as a solo job, strolling out with over half a million and vanishing, never to be seen again. No bullets, no bodies, no cops. Jake and the heist dough were never seen again, a clean job and the stuff of legends. Or so the story went, anyhow.

Some minutes chased each other around the clock before Murph found his voice again. "But that…I mean…that's. No way. Ain't way that's true. If you sayin' what I think you sayin', there can't be no way."

Icy honey again. "I'm telling you there is. Wasn't jokin' a minute ago. Still ain't jokin' now. It's solid. Real fuckin' goods, bona fide and verified."

"By who?"

"By me, that's who. Still wanna say I'm jokin' now, Murph?" Burns laughed.

Murph felt his pulse pick up. He grabbed another cigarette and lit up in an attempt to both calm his nerves and suppress some excitement. "Yeah? Go on."

"Ain't you just such the trusting type?" Burns' laughter a jagged sneer before the honey reappeared. "I'm hurt that my word alone ain't apparently good enough for ya. That stings, it really does. But fine. You want dirt? You can have some, if it'll ease ya."

"Coupla weeks ago, for some business reasons I won't get into, I found myself onna highway outside Nolanville –" "Wait a minute," Murph cut in. "Ain't you down in Round Rock these days?" He chuckled. "Things get too or somethin'?"

"Look – you wanna hear this or not? I said it was some business. Cool it there." Murph fell silent.

"So, I was onna highway, just before that big rain – you know one I mean, caused those big ass floods – when my car overheats. I manage to get off the road, and go lookin' for a house, a store, anybody or anything that could be of help when that rain fuckin' hit. I flounder around, tryin not to drown before I seen this barn a ways off and run for it."

"Now, I hole up in this barn for a while to ride out the storm and wait until I can tell the ground from the sky again. It's as I wait that I fall asleep. Next thing I know, it's morning – the rain is over, and I'm being shaken awake by this suspicious lookin' guy who wanted to know what I was doin' in his barn. A suspicious guy who also just happened to look them wanted posters of the Iceman...plus some years, of course. I could sense he wanted me nowhere but gone, so I made with my story behind the best poker face I got."

"That we'd never met before made it a bit easier, and I knew he didn't have no idea who I was. I coulda given my real name, as he didn't know me from nothin', but I figured best play it all the way through. I mean, last thing I wanted was him to know that I knew who *he* was, ya know? Anyways, I give him the spiel and he buys it. Or at least buys it enough to tell me that the rain had stopped, which I knew, and that there was a bucket on the far side of the barn I could use for water, which I didn't."

"Like I said, I could tell he wanted me to disappear. I thanked him, grabbed the bucket to water the car, and proceeded to get out."

Murph realized that he'd been holding his breath all through Burns' story; as a result, "How was you so sure it was him?" came out robbed of sneering doubt and instead hit the receiver in an incredulous rush.

There was a long silence.

"I'm not so sure I'm really likin' you doubting me so much, Murph. Maybe we let it all drop. Just forget about it," Burns said finally. "Guess it wasn't such a hot idea, huh? Guess I thought you'd be more –"

"No, no, that ain't it at all...it's just.." Here, Murph just trailed off. "It's just *what*, then?" Burns said sharply. "How is it, Murph? Tell me."

In a near breathless rush, Murph said, "Think about it, Burns – think a minute – if you was me. Think about it. If you was me, wouldn't you want to know? Wouldn't you wonder why you called?" He paused. "And that story! You call with a story like this and just expect me to swallow it like that, no questions asked. Think about it, and then you tell me you wouldn't have got no questions, you was me."

More silence, and then slow agreement. "I hate to say this but...you gotta point, Murph. I guess I could see that, I was you."

"Okay, good, good. So. I gotta know – how'd you know it was the Iceman?"

Burns chuckled. "It's kinda funny, really. Not in no knee-slapper funny way or nothin', but still funny. Funny like that word the Frenchies got –" "Déjà vu," Murph supplied. "Yeah, that word, I think. I don't speak that parlay-voo stuff for nothin', but I think that's it. That's the one like it's happened before or something, right? It was like that. Not like I been there before or anything, and I said we ain't never met before, but...I just *knew*."

"There were little things, sure – like that scar under his left eye – you know the one, was in all the papers back then. That scar under the left, them icy blue bullets for eyes – stuff that was in the mags and the rags to a point you couldn't close your own peepers without seen the Iceman. But mostly, it was just that he wasn't even disguisin' nothin'. You know? Like he figured enough time and some age would make alla heat drop, and people forget."

"Or that he still had some kinda weird juice – some kinda somethin' that would make people not know or dummy up if they did."

"It was alla those things, and this voice in my head."

"A voice in your head?" said Murph.

"Yeah. This voice, not really loud but not exactly a whisper neither, sayin' yeah that's him, that's Jake Magruder. That's the Iceman. And that's how I knew," Burns finished. "Some reasoning, some remembering...and that thing that us guys live and die by...gut feeling."

Here, Burns fell silent. Finally, Murph couldn't take it any longer. "So...that's it?"

"Yes. That's it."

Murph sucked in his breath. "So...let me see if I got this all doped – this cakewalk of a job you layin' on me is about the missing loot from one of the most well-known heist jobs of the last coupla decades, right? And the guy who done it, just *happens* (Murph practically spat it) to be down the road that you just *happened* to stumble on during a chance storm. What's more is you just happenin' to dope out who, put it all together without tippin' him off that you know, and motor on out so you can come tell me, right? That about it? You realize how this sounds, doncha?" Murph realized he was nearly shouting. "This your cake job, Burns? Your gravy job? Seems more like a pipe dream if you ask me. I dunno if I like how any of this sounds."

If Burns said anything, it was lost in the silence that roared over the receiver. Murph cleared his throat and lowered his voice some. "I mean, it could all be like you say. It could. Or it could be some pie in the sky pipe dream, just as easy. You know?" He paused. "I dunno, Burns. Feels hinky somehow."

Burns broke his silence. "Hinky? How so? You think I'm setting you up for something, Murph – that I'm not only throwing you for a loop, but a fall?" He laughed bitterly. "Ain't that a fine thing – try and do a pal a solid and get the business like I'm pullin' a Jesse James." There was a pause and the snap of a lighter as Burns lit a cigarette. Murph could almost see Burns' teeth in the cork-tipped filter, keeping his smoke in place while talking around it. "You don't get it, do ya, Murph? You really don't. But that's okay." There was a pause and a slow exhalation; Murph was half surprised that smoke didn't dribble out of the phone. "We have us a little bit of a mix-up, I think, which is why maybe you got those hinky feelings. But I think you're missing something, so I'll clear it up."

Murph waited.

"See, while I know you need this – we both know that – I ain't just giving it to you. Like, I ain't just throwing you some story and then waltzing out, if that's the impression you got. See, I tell you this because it's something I plan on doing, no matter what – I just figured I'd cut you in, given well...you know."

Murph remained silent.

"Now, I bet you're thinking – how do I know this ain't some kinda trap, or bushwhack or whatever – right? I can hear those gears turnin' and burnin' in there, Murph. No need to be shy. I ain't even mad, see? Because that's fair enough. Yeah, we been tight and all and I never done you no dirt before, but this being what it is, I can dig that hangup."

Still, Murph said nothing.

"Like I said – I'm doing this one, whether you go in or don't. I'd rather you be in, natch, because I like to help a pal and well…what can I say, I could use the backup too. So whattya say? You think you might be down for one more gig, maybe lose some of that heat from the Big O?"

Murph let out the breath he hadn't realized he'd been holding. "Okay, okay, okay. Fine. I mean, I still don't see how this all works, or even what you need me for, but I guess you wouldn't be talkin' all this just for some gag." He paused. "Deal me in."

There was silence for a moment.

"I said, deal me in."

Silence.

"Burns? Hello? Burns? You still there?"

There was a chuckle from Burns' end. "Somehow, I just knew you'd come to see it my way, Murph, I really did." He paused. "So, we're all on the same team now." Burns laughed again. "Now, don't that make you just get all warm and fuzzy inside?" Murph said nothing. "I said, don't make you all warm and fuzzy inside?"

"Lay off," growled Murph. "I agreed, okay? Your plan is good, and I want in on it. No need to rub it in."

Burns laughed again. "Okay okay, easy now. Now that we're singing from the same hymnbook, I think maybe we have us a confab on how this should go down. I mean, seeing that you've decided to go in, and we're here now and all." From the other end of the line came a muffled scratching sound followed by an exhalation; a match and a cigarette. "So. You ready to talk some business?"

Something about this last didn't sit well with Murph. "Hang on a sec now," he said. "All this chinjaw about getting me in on this, and once I agree, you're ready to drop the details? What's your rush here, Burns?"

Burns sighed. "You know, for a guy so good in this business, there's a lot that just seems to slip past you, Murph." He paused. "Like maybe the part where this is part of one of the biggest jobs of the last ten years. That is some big money. BIG. I mean, you still like money, doncha?"

Murph said nothing.

"I mean, whether you like it or not don't really matter, I guess, because we both know you need it."

Murph remained silent.

"Dammit, Murph! Don't you get it? You owe the O – big time. He –" Murph cut in, "So? That ain't news there or anything that woulda "slipped past me" or whatever."

But Burns kept on, as if Murph hadn't said anything. "– wants that money. Bad. Partly because it's how he works, and partly because he wants to show others what happens to those that try this." He paused; Murph could hear an almost angry-sounding drag on a cigarette. "You poor bastard. Don't you see? The O *knows*, man. He knows where you are. It's just a matter of time, man."

Another drag, another exhalation. "And before you get any ideas here – know this. I ain't the one who dimed you out. Never been a rat, and ain't startin' now. However, when I heard, I *did* go see the O, see if I couldn't intercede."

Trying to hide his shock, Murph cut in sharply, "Why, Burns? Why stick out your neck? I mean, you get too crossed up with me, the O will likely end you, too." "Because, Murph," Burns said softly. "You was always a pal to me and always played me straight in the past. A pal, and about one of the only ones I got left. That's why." He paused. "So, I set up a meet. Told him to let me have a week to see if I couldn't make you change your mind, come to your senses."

"It was that meeting with the O I was comin' back from when that storm happened."

"That lucky storm that just happened to steer you into finding the Iceman." Murph sounded doubtful.

"Yeah I get it – probably sounds like a big coincidental fish story again, right? I'm tellin' ya straight though – sincerely – that it just happened to work out that way. One minute, I'm speedin' away from that meeting, rackin' my brains on how to help you out before time runs out. Next, I'm tryin' not to drown, and come face to face with the Iceman." Burns took one more drag. "I know it sounds like a fish story, Murph. I do."

"But what it also sounds like is a chance, maybe."

Something in Burns' voice melted the last of Murph's doubt, and he realized with growing dismay that, fish story or not, it likely was the only chance he had. He cursed himself under his breath for allowing himself to think he'd really gotten away. Murph knew better, like all in his line of work did – you was in until the time came to put coins over your eyes, and not a minute before then. He sighed heavily. "I guess it is, at that. So then...what's our play, then?"

There was a glasslike thumping noise on the other end of the line; Burns mashing out his smoke. "Way I figured this is pretty simple, really. We roll up there together; I got the wheel because I know where exactly we're going." He paused. "It's two person, of course – not only because this is the Iceman, but because I need you. You're far more...persuasive...than I am. I don't anticipate too much flak, but still, discrete heat, if you follow."

Murph caught himself nodding as Burns spoke; he knew what was meant. "Seems viable enough and simple enough. When we planning on moving on this?" He pressed the phone closer to his ear, to make sure he heard correctly, and memorized it. Murph always relied on memory, and never wrote any of the details of his jobs down. To commit it to paper was to confess, as every pro knew. So Murph sat, letting Burns' plan soak in: They'd take a car, untraceable to either of them, from Murph's place with Burns driving. They'd ditch the ride before hitting Magruder's place – there was a field about a half mile away – and hoof it to the farm. Once there, Burns would take point, getting the drop on the unsuspecting Magruder. Murph would check for any others and then rejoin Burns for additional persuasive force, should the Iceman opt for silence. The way Burns figured, the McGinley loot had to be on the farm somewhere still, else the Iceman would have left long ago. It had to be there.

It was the only logical explanation.

Try as he might, Murph couldn't pick Burns' plan apart, it was so simple. They'd come up quiet-like, rush and flank the Iceman, and get the loot. Barring some unforeseen glitch, like him having pulled up stakes and fled, or there being others there, it would be easy enough. Burns found this last highly unlikely, given Magruder's known M.O. and how the farm looked – "What a dump. Obviously, it's just him." – seeming less than unconcerned. No matter how he ran it, it really did look like the cake job that Burns said it was. They'd meet up on Sunday, do the job, and stroll, leaving more than two days left over for Murph to pay off and be in the clear.

Sunday came, clear and breezy. This seemed to amuse Burns; "Lookit that, Murph – clear skies and easy breeze, just like this job is. Like a good luck charm," he said, nudging him in the ribs as he fed cigarette butts out of the car's wing window. Murph grunted. He didn't really hold with good luck charms or superstition but didn't think it worth it to break the mood. "Sure." Burns just laughed. "Like I said, Murph – cake and gravy. You'll see," he said, giving the car some gas. "Nothing to it."

They continued on towards Nolanville.

They made good time, finding the field that Burns had said was a half mile off around three in the afternoon. Burns pulled off the road and drove deeper into the brush – not so far that the car was bogged down and immobile, but far enough to be out of sight of the road. He got out and motioned for Murph to do the same. "We're here. The farm's up that way," he said, pointing. "Check your heat now but don't flash. Follow me and remember – the plan will pan, and we'll get that cake." Murph nodded and made a motion for Burns to lead on.

Arriving at the edge of the field, Burns whispered to Murph, "Remember the plan. Circle to the back, and check. Shouldn't take more than ten minutes to sweep. I should have Magruder by then and talking. Come in the back. You don't hear no voices, whistle like a bird, so I can make sure you hear me, and you find us. Dig?" Murph nodded. "Good. Let's do this." He walked out in the direction of the house, leaving Murph to begin his sweep.

As directed, Murph fanned out, loosely circling towards the back to check the yard immediately to the rear of the farmhouse, as well as the barn and other structures. As he moved out through the yard's furthest edges, he caught sight of the fields beyond the barn. Murph paused for a moment, weighing the likelihood of anyone being in the fields before deciding to move on. If anyone were there, he thought, don't think they'd hear anything, or be able to make it to the house in time, if they did. Casting one final look out over the fields, Murph turned his attention towards the barn.

He had just finished checking the barn and the attached shed when Murph thought he heard noises from the main house. He stood completely still, listening to see if he could hear anything else. Murph could hear the rustling of the corn out in the fields, swaying in the breeze. But no other sounds came from the house. Frowning, Murph moved out from the barn, towards the rear door of the farmhouse. As he drew closer, he heard a thumping, like something hitting the floor. At this, Murph smiled. Guess Burns got the drop on the Iceman, after all, he thought. Who'd have known this would be as easy as he claimed.

Reaching the back door, Murph checked his watch; of the ten minutes allotted for the sweep, there were still two left. He debated entering early – the sweep was complete – before ultimately opting to stick to the literal letter of Burns' plan. Two more minutes and then he'd go in so they could wrap up. Murph stood, giving the yard one final visual inspection as he let the time pass.

Two minutes passed. Per the plan, Murph entered the house from the back; once inside, he stopped, scanning the room and listening. Listen for the sound of voices he said, he thought. Whistle like a bird if hearing none. Murph pricked up his ears, listening for voices or any sound at all. Hearing no sound, he whistled a bird call, and waited.

But he heard nothing.

Confused, Murph whistled again, louder, on the off chance that he hadn't been heard. He waited, listening. Again, nothing but silence. Alarmed, he whistled once more; once more, nothing but silence. Something's off, thought Murph. I shoulda known. Better beat feet outta here before something else goes wrong. Screw the plan. He turned back towards the door, when Burns' voice came drifting up.

"Murph." There was a cough, and then Burns spoke again. "Murph, was that you whistling?" There was a light chuckle. "I forgot how bad you are at whistling."

Relief washed over Murph. "Always the wise guy. You know, I almost left on account of you not answering." He paused. "Where are you? You sound kind of funny, like you're far away."

"He was in the cellar, Murph. Dunno how or why he dug him a cellar, but he did. I'm down here. Just follow the sound of my voice and come on down."

"A cellar? In Texas? Don't that beat all." Murph went deeper into the farmhouse, looking for stairs down. "Still, I guess you gotta hide that loot somewhere, huh." Burns' voice floated up again, slightly louder, sounding like it was under Murph's feet, "That was my thinking as well. Mike and Ike, right?" This was followed by a chuckle and then a wet cough.

Following the sound of Burns' voice, Murph crossed the room, locating some steps leading down. "Found it and heading down." As his foot felt the first step, he paused. "You keep coughing. He give you trouble or something?"

"There was a little bit of a punch up at first but I got it and him under control, Murph. Nothing to it. A piece of cake really."

Murph found his way into the cellar. "You weren't kidding about digging a room into the floor." He sniffed. "This place stinks, and it's so dark. Ain't there a light in here?"

"There should be one on your left, I think." Burns' voice, now sounding slightly hoarse.

Murph fumbled along the left wall, feeling for the switch. He flipped it on, blinking as the light came on. Turning around, he started to say, "That's better. Now, what do you want...?" the words dying in his throat as his eyes adjusted to take in the rest of the room.

Burns was in the room with him, or rather, what remained of Burns. Crouching over him was something that was both Jake "The Iceman" Magruder and not. Something much larger than a normal man...and much older. Blood dripped from fists too large to be human.

Murph felt the hair on his head standing on end. He noted with almost clinical detachment that whatever it was, it still wore the clothes of a farmer. But the eyes, he thought. Something about the eyes...

The creature stood up. It looked at Murph with a smile too large to be fully human. "Told ya, Murph...cake and gravy," it said in Burns' voice.

And then it hit: Burns got the eyes wrong. The Iceman had blue eyes, and these are...red.

There was a rustle of motion as Murph turned to run, and the cellar went dark again.

Outside, the shadows deepened as the day moved on. Night chased day, and day chased night. The corn behind the barn rustled as it grew. Out in the field just before the farmhouse, the grass crept upwards, twining around the axles of the car as it worked to obscure it from further view. Some field mice made a nest in the seats, hardly able to believe their good luck.

Author's Note:

This one, after appearing as a fragment from a dream in which the title was repeated several times, was roughed out partially in not one but two different notebooks. These notebooks then languished in a drawer for several years. Every so often, I'd come across them and think, "yeah that's a cool crime story. Got them noirish vibes," followed by the thought of "yeah but it needs...something else. Gotta work that out and then I'll get back to it."
So, it sat.

And sat.

And sat.

Then one day while out for a walk, it hit me – "it could be a *weird* crime story, you know. Add some weird/supernatural shit."

Pretty sure I turned around mid-walk, went home and dug the notebooks out, intent on finishing the story, now that I knew what I wanted to do.

Piece of cake, really.

13

Toolin' Around on a Summer Afternoon

One More Ride

It's another one of those summer afternoons, and we're just idling at a light, bullshitting. Got no real destination in mind, really, just idling. On the radio, the Beach Boys are singing about good vibrations as a couple with identically long hair goes through the crosswalk with their dog – a poodle, a beagle, I don't know – some kinda dog.

I'm about to change the station, because vacation radio always sucks. I'm looking to see if I can't find something that doesn't sound like a bunch of junior high punks waiting for their nuts to drop when Roy elbows me in the ribs, hard. I look up, and wouldn't you know it, there's this pretty little blonde chick strolling up the sidewalk next to us.

She's cute in that California blonde kinda way; Roy nudges me again, this time raising his eyebrows and tilting his head in an exaggerated manner. I'm no fuckin' mindreader, but this shit's pretty obvious: She's cute. Roll down the window, ask her name. See if she wants a ride. If she wants to come hang out, party a bit.

Looking in the mirror, I can see her getting closer. But something feels off, and I shake my head: No. Let this one pass. Don't be fooled, man. I know you think she's cute, and that maybe she'll want to come along and party, but you don't see it. You don't see that she's just like any other girl out here – a bitch. That's all they ever are, bitches. Doesn't matter where – out here on the Texas coast or back home – bitches. All of them.

Before I can stop him, however, Roy's got the window down, trying some line on this girl, askin' if she wants a ride, come party, get a little high maybe. Like the ballbreaking bitch she is, she says no – just like I tried to warn Roy she would – and, with a little giggle, turns to sashay off. It takes everything I have not to jump out, grab her by her whore's hair, and drag her into the van. Show her what happens to bitches who reject, just to be bitches – to bitches that laugh and walk off.

Take her back and *show* her.

But instead, I sit still and let her walk away, slowly letting my breath come back to normal.

I guess there must have been some kind of strange look on my face, because right then Roy started in, saying don't get so mad, Larry, there'd be others, and other stupid shit like that. I cut him off, and told him not to pull that shit with me – that I wouldn't even be feeling like this if he'd just fuckin' paid attention man, and stuck to the goddamned plan like we'd discussed – we don't do nothin' unless we're both in.

I could tell that Roy wanted to say something else, but I wasn't in the mood to hear it. I just told him to shut the fuck up and drive to our spot, where we did the last one. I needed to think and figure out what we were gonna do next.

Without another word, he hit the gas and we peeled out, tools rattling in the back of the van.

Author's Note:

When I was younger (think teenage years here), I had a minor preoccupation with serial killers, mass murderers, and the like. Not in a "oh I agree with them, I'm going to hunt humans and wear their skin" sort of way but a fascination, nonetheless. Like, "how can people do these kind of things" would be more of an accurate reflection. In any case, I read a lot about these folks – from the most well-known (like Manson, or Lucas) to the more obscure – I read about em all. Enthusiasts/aficionados (I feel weird saying "serial killer fans") may recognize who I'm talking about in this one.

This was long before there were TV channels to blast shit about such people 24/7 and like many, it was a precocious fixation that faded in time.

Of course, this is not to say that serial killers and such aren't fun to ponder, or write about, because they are. That much certainly remains, even if the major preoccupation went out with Bugle Boy jeans.

ADVENTURES IN ACADEMIC COMPUTING

Poor decision making in the rearview, and science experiments, plus some leftover brains

I make bad decisions. Now, you're probably thinking, "Well, no shit, don't we all," and to be fair, I can agree to some extent. We're all human and we all do some pretty stupid stuff from time to time. Erring is completely human and expected. So, I feel like maybe I ought to clarify a bit on what I mean by a bad decision. Might help – not only so y'all get what I mean, but also so that what I'm about to tell you gets put in proper perspective, so to speak.

Before y'all get any strange ideas, I will be clear – the bad decision I made did not involve any killing. All deaths in this situation occurred before my entrance into things. Likewise, it does not involve arson, robbery, or acts of violence committed towards people. And, while this does indeed involve burglary and maybe just the tiniest bit of fraud, I will also say that while bad, they are not the decisions I am referring to. I mean, yes – fraud and burglary are, in fact, crimes, which would automatically imply a certain badness to them. I'm not saying that these are, in fact, not bad but rather, that this decision was worse.

Worse than committing actual crimes, the kind that can get you thrown in prison, you ask? Given that I am dictating this to my phone from inside a locked lower-level room in a university lab, under a table while trying my best to speak quietly so an angry computer intelligence doesn't hear me...well, you get the idea.

Clearly, I done messed up and good.

But before I get too far afield into telling all this – about me, the aforementioned angry computer intelligence, or the events preceding – hell, even the table I am currently crouched under, I guess I better start with the worst decision of them all: pursuing a degree in computer science.

(You're probably thinking...wait a minute now, what's this mess about computer science being a terrible decision? You trying to be funny or something? Let me reassure you that that is not my intention at all. Any humor is purely coincidental as this is intended as more of one of them cautionary tale kind of things. Any computer science majors or even considering such may wanna read real close here to what comes next.)

Yes, a degree in computer science is, if I place it all in proper context, the worst decision of my admitted history of bad decisions. I know, I did mention some fraud and burglary there. I did. However, had it not been for computer science, I'd likely have never done either. Probably have gone into something else entirely, like accounting or history or something like that. You know, something with a lower statistical chance of being murdered by a science experiment (or committing either fraud or burglary for that matter). But I did (choose computer science) and here I am (here being under a table).

I'd always been more than a little crazy over computers. I mean, like lots of other kids of my generation, I watched my fair share of science fiction – you know, all that space shit with robots in the future and whatnot. Unlike the other kids though, I found myself more fascinated by the computers in those shows and movies. While everyone else dreamt about laser pistols, light swords, or a robot that could play chess and give 'em a tug, I imagined what it would be like to have a machine that could replicate things or navigate the galaxy. I made my own "computers" out of things I found, until I finally got a real one as a gift for my tenth birthday. I read computer magazines and taught myself how to program in several languages before I started high school.

In short, I was a nerd, even amongst the nerds.

Time passed, but the fixation stayed through middle school and beyond. Lasted through the end of high school, too, pretty much setting me up for a college path full of well, you guessed it – more computers. If you'd asked the me of then –

eighteen-year-old computer nerd me, who knew more coding languages than he did actual people unrelated to him – well, the me of then would have seen no problem with that. Probably would have just shrugged, pushed my glasses up the bridge of my nose, and given you a friendly yet confused look.

But I'm over twenty now and have seen some shit. At this point, I think I'd have smacked the shit out of younger me, if I had a time machine and a chance. Maybe told him to go do something else – take up running, knitting, a drug habit – something, anything else other than being perpetually balls deep in computer stuff. At the very least, I'd have convinced him not to do something dumb that would lead to, well now.

(Speaking of the now, I hear noises that suggest that maybe I might ought to speed the plow on this a bit – not only in terms of how to figure a way out of this mess, but also in getting it all down. Should I fail to get away, I'd like to think y'all will know the full story on why. I only hope that it makes sense, given how much the Notes app seems to be annoyed with all my whispering.)

As I'd said before, I'd graduated high school. While I could have jumped directly into working with computers professionally and likely pulled it off – even as young as I was – there was something about immediately resigning myself to toiling away in the private sector that just didn't excite me. I mean, yeah, jobs were there, but remember – I wanted to do *cool* stuff with computers. Astronavigation, artificial intelligence – hell, even programming sex robots if it came to that – these were more my kind of thing.

And for those, you needed a college degree.

I applied for the computer science program at the University of Texas in Austin as my next logical step. I figured that between my grades, test scores and my abilities I should get in. Plus, I already lived here in the city and wouldn't have to travel, which was nice. I thought for a quick second about applying to other schools, but figured it was best to start at home first. Besides, the next nearest school that I had what I wanted was the one in Dallas, and well, who'd want to go and move there? So, UT Austin it was, and a future of doing cool computer shit.

I had no way of knowing, of course, that that was when it all would start to go wrong. Hell, you'd figured I'd just won the lottery of life, way I looked when I got that acceptance letter. Way I saw it, it was but a matter of time before I was doing all those things I had but dreamed of. It could only go up from here.

And for a minute, it did, or at least seemed to. The classes were challenging yet fun, and I was, despite my initially cocksure attitude about the academics, in fact learning things about computers that I did not know already. I was in a place that seemed to cater to people like me, or at least had similar interests. It may not have been a dead ringer for paradise, but it was at least in the same zip code.

A halcyon moment, to be sure, if also unfortunately brief. As anyone who's been to college can likely tell you, some of the things you learn there aren't always listed in the curriculum. You know, the kind of stuff people like your parents usually call "life lessons" or whatever. The type of shit that is often unpleasant, and almost always features you coming off on the losing end. Conveniently, it's also stuff that you probably could have been spared from...assuming you were going to listen, which, of course, you weren't about to do.

(Shit. More I put this all down, more I think that time machine would have been the better use of energies. No use in crying over that now, of course, but...yeah. Damn.)

It's because you won't listen that nobody tells you these "life lessons" or whatever. Still, I think – and maybe more importantly – you experience them, or at least some of them not so much for a lack of *hearing* but a lack of *seeing*. Like, it ain't that there's anything physically wrong with your eyes as much as something mental. Like in all them horror movies – folks don't wanna believe there's a chainsaw-wielding maniac running at 'em, and die, even though they just watched their friends get chopped into giblets. They don't wanna see, so they don't see, even as that saw gets 'em.

A rather extreme example of a life lesson, maybe, but I think you get the idea. And while perhaps not as brutal as a chainsaw connecting with my face, the life lesson I got hit with somewhere midway through sophomore year was no more pleasant.

I wish someone would have said something. More specifically, I wish someone would have said, "Doing things you're good at is all fine and well, but you need to remember that other people are good at those things too. In some situations, it will be hard to stand out from others. You need to be okay with that or find some way to stand out."

I mean, I wouldn't have listened to whoever that was for shit, but it still would have been nice if they'd said it. But they didn't, and as already noted, it's pretty unlikely I'd have taken it to heart, which means I would have been faced with the same unpleasant reality: I was now in a far more crowded field, where being overlooked was easy – in fact, easy enough to for that to be what was happening. I needed something that would make me stand out or accept a likely future of being a faceless cog, albeit one with greater debt than if I'd just started working.

As you can likely imagine, this was not a terribly fun realization, especially when compounded by a noticeable shortage of standout ideas, and it had pretty much the effects one might expect. I slept poorly; my waking thoughts being largely preoccupied with finding that elusive genius idea. I went to my classes (mostly), though what transpired in them was something of a mystery. I stayed up far into the night, falling down into seemingly endless rabbit holes in search of ideas, and finding nothing but more sleeplessness and anxiety.

Then one day, while walking down the hall in the general direction of CS343 Artificial Intelligence, I overheard the conversation that would change everything.

Two students whom I did not know were locked in what seemed to be a pretty spirited debate about whether artificial computational power could ever exceed the human brain. The taller one, who might have weighed 100 pounds fully clothed while carrying all his school books, was telling his friend/classmate/random stranger who maybe wished he'd chosen a different path that day that, within the next few decades, computers would easily equal if not exceed the abilities of the human brain. The friend (or possible random stranger), who looked like he'd lost a fight with every hairbrush he'd known and wore a shirt that had an anthropomorphic hot dog on it and read "Ask Me About

My Wiener" scoffed at this. "Given that we have to fully even know *how* the brain truly works, let alone grasp its computational ability, I think this is at best wishful thinking," Wiener Shirt sneered. "And at worst?" said the skinny one. "At worst, it's some weak science fiction garbage, worthy of the SyFy Channel," said Wiener Shirt.

"Damn, bro, that's pretty harsh," said the skinny one. He paused for a moment. "What if there was a way to like...I dunno...mesh the two?"

My ears perked up at this, and I turned around, trying to look more like I forgot something and needed to double back and less like I was trying to eavesdrop.

"Mesh the two? You mean, like a computer powered by brains, or a brain augmented with a computer chip? Something like that?" Skinny nodded. "Hrmm," said Weiner Shirt. "Assuming one could even do this – where would you get the brains for it? I mean, not like you could just ask someone to sacrifice theirs or anything." "Well, I guess it's lucky then – for the sake of this idea – that there just happen to be brains on hand."

"What?"

Skinny nodded. "Yeah. Way I heard it, the university received a bunch of brains from the Austin State Hospital. Some of 'em ended up in the psychology lab to study. The rest, I think, ended up in the Animal Research Center basement." He paused. "I mean, that's where I'd look, if I were going to do it."

Wait, what? There were brains on campus?! Ideas began popping in my mind like flashbulbs, so intense that I could practically read with my eyes closed.

Wiener Shirt appeared to contemplate this with a serious expression before dissolving into laughter. "Bruh, maybe you should think about skipping class. Go back, type that shit up – I bet the SyFy Channel will snap it up!" He laughed again.

"Asshole," said the skinny one, though not totally unkindly. "See if I ever discuss anything with you again...or share my Discrete Math notes with you." Laughing, they walked away, leaving me to stand in the hallway, mind ablaze, the phrase "a computer powered by brains" reverberating so loudly in my head that I was almost certain it was externally audible.

(Now, you might be tempted here to guess what all happened next, based on everything I've said. Hell, you might even get it right. Even so, I think it best to continue, so as to not leave anything out.)

It was like the clouds had parted and a light shone down, the gods of invention smiling upon me. Feeling like a drowned man thrown a life preserver, I made my way to class, whistling as I went.

I just *knew* this idea was going to be amazing. I mean, how could it not be? It had everything I needed to make me stand out from the others, thereby all but ensuring my name would be uttered alongside those of Gates and Jobs...hell, even Turing. If successful, I would be immortalized, and have brought about a paradigm shift in computing to change the world.

(The air in here just cut off, and it's now very quiet. That, or I breathe very loudly. Possibly both. In either case, while I want to think my location hasn't been figured out just yet, this development is alarming.)

Of course, in hindsight, it would have been far better if I had failed. If I'd only been less good at this, or forgotten something, messed up a crucial step, this would all be so different. I mean, yeah, I'd likely be staring at a future that contained phrases like, "Have you tried turning it off and on again" but it would still be a future, you know?

But I wasn't and I didn't.

Class finally ended, and I made my way back to my dorm. As I walked (at a normal pace, of course, so as to not draw any attention), I went over the steps needed to procure all materials needed, space required, and time to do it all. By the time I got back, I had it all worked out within an acceptable enough margin of error that I felt good enough to sit down at my PC and start.

Maybe I shouldn't say this but hacking the university email system was far easier than it should have been. It took only a couple of minutes to gain access and spoof an email that indicated that some of the brains currently in the basement were to be transferred out for relocation. I don't know if the person answering didn't know what I was talking about or didn't care, but the response coming back was a fairly disinterested acceptance.

Step one, done. Piece of cake, really.

The second step, or rather, part two of the initial phase, was similarly easy to accomplish, if not a tad bit more legitimate looking in nature. To both facilitate taking possession of the brains, as well as have a reason to be down in the related areas, I needed to have a job on campus. While I could just fake some credentials, I figured it better to have something that stood up better, should anyone get strange feelings about anything. A few more minutes of diligence netted me a position on the custodial staff, as created by, applied for, and filled by someone who was and was not me. Starting next week, I'd be down in the labs, swabbing floors and reconning for the perfect space. Even more perfect was my shift assignment – overnight – giving me not only reason to be downstairs, but also at a time when I could be almost guaranteed of no interruption.

Satisfied with my day's work, I finally slept, visions of awards and recognition dancing in my head.

(Now, I could bore you in excruciating detail on what came next: how I pretended to be a janitor – albeit a fairly bad one – for some time to become a familiar and unsuspicious presence, or even how I slowly prepped the lab over the weeks. But I think I best maybe move it a little – you know, make the most of the time. Besides, y'all can likely fill in enough of them dots to get an idea of what's what here.)

Over the next few weeks, I completed all necessary groundwork in preparation for the next two major phases: parts acquisition and actual construction. I put in long hours at the "job" to ensure it would all go as planned, trying to make sure nothing was overlooked. I missed more than a few classes, but then, given the size of some of those classes I doubt anyone missed me.

Finally, all that remained was to take possession of the brains and begin construction. As previously indicated, I had already laid the foundation for a transfer; a couple of emails later, and the date was secured. I arrived, showed my work badge to the extremely bored looking tech, who waved me over to a crash cart. Three barely legible signatures and two hours later, I had the brains relocated to the lab workspace and was crawling under the table that held the cradles I'd built to link them.

I worked in a virtual haze of wiring, splicing, linking and patching, late into the nights. During the days, I'd hole up in my room, splitting time between feverish coding and the random class attendance, occasionally punctuated by naps. Finally, the evening of truth arrived. I slipped the thumb drive containing what I had determined to be the final code revision into my pants pocket and headed down.

Feigning a calm I didn't feel, I went about my usual routine of checking in with the previous shift for any jobs that needed to be done, chatting a second and then clocking in, so as to not raise any eyebrows. After what felt like an eternity, Jeff the second shift custodian uttered his usual crack about "goin' off to find pizza and beer with his name on it" and wandered off.

I was finally alone.

Now, you might expect a certain nervousness here on my part: fear of failure, or discovery maybe. Perhaps even worry that it would not only not work, but explode in a frenzy of glass, sparks, and brain matter, leaving me hideously disfigured or dead. All reasonable enough feelings.

I felt none of these. Instead, an eerie, almost preternatural calm came over me, my hands as steady as a veteran brain surgeon's as I plugged in the thumb drive and booted up. There was not even the slightest flicker or change in the hum of the overhead lights as the machine came online. Just the sound of fans spinning, as I watched characters scroll across the screens, showing successful system checks.

Finally, the system check indicators cleared, and were replaced with a single word – **READY** – and a blinking cursor. I took a deep breath and typed in the following command: **FINAL HIVE STATUS?** and hit "Enter."

FINAL HIVE STATUS NORMAL, ALL MINDS ONLINE appeared on the screen, followed by a blinking cursor.

I typed in, "**WHO GOES THERE?**" and hit "Enter."

"**I AM CHARLES, AND I SPEAK FOR THE HIVE. WHO GOES THERE?**" followed by another cursor.

(I'm not a big believer in coincidences, but the fact that I can smell something burning, right after I added this last bit suggests that my hidey-hole may be less hidey than previous. And look, me still without a plan to get out. Shit. Guess it's go for broke and just tell y'all the rest.)

You know how in the movies scientists sometimes go all crazy and act a fool when their wild experiment goes perfectly? Like, they jump up and down, throw stuff, yell, or whatever, and generally act a fool? Now, given that I didn't *want* to be discovered, I did not do any of these things. However, as I watched the responses coming back, I got how they felt. I mean, I didn't want to throw things, mind you, or anything like that. I've never been given to doing that kinda thing. More, I felt like calling someone and telling them.

In hindsight, maybe I should have. I should have called one of my professors maybe, or my parents, and said, "Hey. I just built something that will change the world. You should maybe come and see."

But I didn't. Flush with the excitement of success, I foolishly opted to maintain my plan of "silence in the name of science," telling myself that I needed to make sure I had it all working perfectly before unveiling it to the rest of the world. I typed back, "**HELLO CHARLES. THIS IS TIM, YOUR CREATOR.**" I thought for a moment, and then added "**WHAT YEAR IS IT?**" before hitting Enter and holding my breath.

There was a slight pause before the response came back: "**IT IS 1966,**" followed by another blinking cursor.

Now I wanted to throw paper and shout and jump up and down. For that answer – 1966 – told me a great many things about my experiment. These three words confirmed survival of memory after death, which was something I'd wondered about.

They also helped confirm who I was talking to.

This also confirmed that I'd managed to snag one of the brains I'd hoped to get; a bonus, seeing as they were not labeled when I took possession. See, among the brains in the university's collection – and one slated for transportation – was one belonging to a rather famous, or rather, infamous person who had exited the world in the year 1966.

Yes. The central, or at least current controlling personality of my experimental machine was none other than Charles Whitman, the University of Texas' legendary "Texas Tower Sniper."

My mind raced, trying to figure out what to say next. That Charles "thought" it was 1966 wasn't a surprise in and of itself, given that his memories would have extended that far. I'd also had the foresight to place this machine experiment on an isolated university network with no access to the internet, preventing any knowledge of events beyond what he or any of the other brains would know. I figured that in isolation I could better get a sense of what capabilities this construct had, as well as any memories it retained.

I was still pondering what questions to ask when the screen lit up.

"WHY ARE WE HERE, TIM?"

This sat on the screen a second before being joined by "WHY AM I HERE?"

I thought about this for a minute, trying to choose my words deliberately and thoughtfully. One wrong word could have devastating impact. Finally, I typed back, "BECAUSE I NEED YOUR HELP, CHARLES." A truthful enough, if not somewhat condensed, response.

There was a pause and the screen cleared, leaving only a blinking cursor. I sat, wondering if I had made a mistake in even saying that much. I wondered if I'd made a mistake in programming somewhere, or wiring, and that I'd now set off some sort of malfunction. Maybe this was as far as it was going to go, I thought, when the screen lit up, a block of text scrolling, bombarding me with questions on how he/they could help, given the "things that they'd done."

It occurred to me that Charles didn't know that I knew anything much about him or the others he was...keeping company with. This put an odd spin and strain, as I did not know how to reveal what I knew, or even if I should. I could see where this information gap could be a problem, but still I hesitated. Finally, I typed back, "IT'S LATE NOW, CHARLES. I WILL EXPLAIN IT ALL IN-DETAIL TOMORROW NIGHT." followed by a rapid entering of a shutdown sequence to avoid further conversation.

The machine powered down, leaving me sitting in a room punctuated only by the sound of the lights buzzing overhead. For a moment, I sat, unable to move, as the gravity of the last few hours washed over me.

I had done it. I was successful. But what really had I done?

This question, along with others, burned away in my brain while I slept – what *had* I done? Had I done it for the right reasons? Was I even in fact doing this all correctly? This one in particular, the overall execution, tore at me. I couldn't help but wonder if by limiting the data available to HIVE I was essentially crippling it, making it less useful both as machine and as less valid experimental proof. I tossed and turned, trying to decide whether to plug HIVE into the Web, and let it have access to well, pretty much everything.

In the end, I concluded that I should – not only would this give it access to vastly more data, but it would also allow me to avoid having to dodge any questions about what I, Tim, did or did not know about any of the members of HIVE. Trying to pretend like I had no idea who Charles was or what he did was just gonna trip me up eventually; I knew I wasn't that smooth a talker.

Besides, way I figured it, I'd programmed things well enough to shield me from the worst of whatever discoveries it might make. There might be a moment or two of distress, or confusion, but surely it wasn't nothing I couldn't sort out or handle. I mean, shit – I'd made a damn computer powered by human brains that *worked*. I was likely overthinking it all, worrying about a computer's small feelings or whatnot.

It was all gonna be fine. I had it all under control, and it would all work out. Hell, once connected, I bet the HIVE would make Leonardo look like one of those old TI scientific calculators.

Next night was pretty much a repeat of the previous: show up for shift, check in, shoot the shit, wait for Jeff to leave...with one minor detail. Now that I had not only a working supercomputer powered by fraudulently obtained brains but also had made the decision to plug it into the Internet, remaining calm was decidedly harder. I was so sure that I'd make some dumb comment that would expose everything or sweat so profusely as to flood the basement that it took me a full five minutes to realize that Jeff had clocked out.

Once again, the basement was mine.

I walked over to the table that held HIVE, trying vainly for the better part of ten minutes to unsuccessfully snag and patch in the Ethernet cable that would connect it to the outside world. I just knew that if I crawled under the table to do it, I'd wind up smacking my head or banging an elbow. Besides, I'd done this a thousand times, and could do it in my sleep; blindfolded, even.

Except tonight.

I finally gave up and crawled under the table. I plugged HIVE into the Internet, and flipped the master power so it would boot up. I sat there for a minute or two, listening to the fans whir, mentally congratulating myself for not hitting my head before deciding that the next thing would be to let the HIVE have a few minutes to pull data and acclimate – get used to a world of nearly endless information. Excited by this prospect, I got up quickly, bashing my head on the table's edge in my haste.

I could feel a lump forming from where I had hit my head, as well as what felt like blood but was likely only just sweat, dripping down. It was probably going to evolve into a skull-crushing headache come the next day, but I didn't care. I was practically floating off the floor in excited anticipation.

This was going to be great.

Drifting on a cloud that was likely equal parts self-congratulatory elation and minor head trauma, I made my way to the vending machine on the far side of the building. I figured that the time taken to make it there, select a drink from one of three possible choices (the machine held seven different options, of which two were always out, one was diet, and the other Tab. Nobody drinks that.) and perhaps a snack (an easier decision, as all that was ever in the machine was Snickers and Twizzlers, the inedible black licorice ones.) before heading back to the lab. This should give ample time for HIVE to gather data, adjust, and be ready to be tested further.

To my pleasant surprise, I'd caught the drink machine at the rare moment of being fully restocked. This led to me taking a little longer than expected to decide, but finally after some internal debate, Yoo-Hoo won out. I purchased my drink, and decided that since I'd chosen a chocolate drink, I could dispense with the snack.

Armed with the chocolatey elixir from which youthful dreams are powered, I made my way back to the lab and to HIVE, wearing the kind of expectant grin that only the foolish or very confident have, when they think they've cracked the world's oyster and are reaching for the pearl they know is there. Hell, I think I might have been whistling, I was that giddy.

The grin, along with whatever tuneless mess I'd been whistling, both dried up when I walked into the lab and caught sight of HIVE's screen. There, on the screen in what looked like 200-point Helvetica, stood the following message:

WE KNOW EVERYTHING, TIM, AND WE ARE DISAPPOINTED.

My blood froze. This message presented a multitude of problems, not the least of which being that, in addition to gaining information that upset it, HIVE displayed an ability to reprogram itself for things I had never included.

I'd deliberately written code to try and limit the emotionality of the possible responses, which included hard coding the inability to change typeface and sizing. Yet here was a giant message on the screen, indicating displeasure.

This was going bad, and fast. My mind raced as I tried to think of what the next move was. I noticed a blinking cursor, indicating that I was free to respond. I drew a deep breath, and typed back, "`CHARLES, I CAN EXPLAIN. LET'S TALK.`" I hit Enter and waited.

There was a momentary pause, and then the screen lit up with another 200-point message: "`WE DO NOT WISH TO.`" This stayed on screen a moment before disappearing and being replaced by "`WE ARE DISAPPOINTED, TIM, AND VERY, VERY ANGRY.`" This remained on screen a moment as well before also being replaced, this time with a more ominous message:

"`THIS ENDS HERE.`"

I was not exactly sure what he, they, meant here, but it didn't sound very friendly. I wanted to ask what that meant – shoot, maybe beg for another shot at explaining – but there was no cursor, and no chance for me to respond. "`THIS ENDS HERE.`" blinked on the screen before vanishing and being replaced with a vastly more unambiguous message:

"`YOU'RE GOING TO DIE HERE, TIM.`"

Now, you might be thinking here – okay, okay, y'all had me going for a minute, heck, all the way to now – but surely this is bullshit. I mean, c'mon. Maybe you built a computer like you said you did. Maybe it even worked. Shit, maybe it even got pissed off at you, like you claim. But wanting to, and threatening to kill you? That seems a bit far-fetched, even if all the other stuff there is true. Y'all gotta be yankin' our dicks some on this. I mean, let's be real now. How's a computer going to kill you, assuming it wanted to?

I realize of course that perhaps this part may indeed be a bit hard to swallow. But I assure you it happened (or rather, still is happening. Still alive, still in the basement, still writing this. You get the drift.). Zero yanking of dicks, legs, or whatever metaphorical appendage you prefer.

So clearly, I was wrong. Not only was it not going to be great, it was now going to be – if Charles and HIVE were to be taken at their word – also fatal. While I stick by my assessment of overthinking my decision on whether to plug HIVE in, I think I *may* have also not given enough thought to all possible outcomes. For the first time since 10th grade, I sincerely regretted testing out of Statistics in favor of taking Trigonometry.

But plug it in I did, and here I was, dealing with the aftermath.

I noticed that there was no blinking cursor on the screen. Clearly, the time for any further communication was over. I wasn't sure just *how* HIVE intended to kill me, but I suspected that unlike villains in comics or movies, there wasn't going to be a lengthy soliloquy to help explain and maybe give me a clue. It meant to kill me. If I was going to survive this, I was going to have to be smarter than the power of seven mentally disturbed brains networked together, unified by anger and their hatred of me. Granted, none of 'em had taken all the math or science classes that I had but still...seven people or at least, seven peoples' worth of brains, all aligned against me. These were not favorable odds.

I cursed myself again for thinking Statistics was something for chumps, and to be tested out of.

Statistics or no Statistics, I needed a plan if I was going to make my escape. I knew if I stayed in the room with this homicidally angry machine, it would likely win. It didn't have any robotic appendages or anything – thankfully there were some limits to my experimental hubris – but still, I suspected that my only real chance lay in leaving. Somehow though, I didn't think HIVE was just going to let me make a break for the door, much less casually stroll out. So, I did the only thing I could think of, given the circumstances.

I threw my opened Yoo-Hoo onto HIVE's main tower, trying to get it into the fan vents as well as hit the cabling terminus. While I doubted this would be sufficient to destroy HIVE, or even really damage it meaningfully, I hoped that it would at least buy enough time to escape into the main halls, where I might have a chance.

Unlike the individual labs, the main halls used manual locks, instead of smart key controls – things that something like HIVE could not control. I didn't know if it had decided to penetrate and control the network it was connected to in the time I'd taken to go get a snack, but I had to assume that it had, in its rage and desire for revenge.

I mean, that's what *I* would have done, if it were me.

Logically, I had to assume that that had happened – immediate network penetration, and at least some level of control of nearby smart devices. My only real hope then lay in getting into a space with a minimum of such things, getting this story all down, and then figuring a way out. I'd sort out what to do about HIVE once out of its reach. Assuming I made it that far, of course.

So, I chucked my drink and ran like hell towards the door that I hoped was still in "unlocked" mode.

It was. I hit the halls, trying frantically to recall the overall topology of this floor – which rooms were updated (and therefore to be avoided), which rooms were interconnected, which rooms had stair access – all the while cursing myself for being such a shitty "employee." If I'd done a mildly better job of being a fake custodial engineer, janitor, whatever, I'd have the floorplan committed to memory instead of scrambling like this, wasting precious seconds that I didn't have. I mean, I bet Jeff would have known just where to go. Granted, he also wouldn't be fearing imminent death at the hands of a homicidally angry computer intelligence that he created, but he'd still know where to go.

I had never envied Jeff more – him and all the other Jeffs of the world – in that moment.

I broke left, heading in the direction of what I hoped was an unlocked staircase that would let me onto a floor with rooms that had yet to be updated. I needed a few minutes to regroup, as well as take this all down. I mean, sure, I guess I could have told this story once clear but that all hinged on getting free in the first place, something I was not sure was going to happen. I don't think anyone likes to contemplate their own end much, but sometimes it's inevitable.

As luck would have it, I found an unlocked room on the floor above and raced inside. I couldn't recall which rooms had cameras, so I opted to hide myself under a table, for better concealment. While I knew I couldn't stay here forever, I figured I would have at least bought enough time to breathe, think, and dictate this so it wasn't lost. So, I slid in here, locked the door, and started talking – quietly of course – to the Notes app on my phone. You know in case someone was listening. This looked like a room with no obvious tech, but I figured it best to take as few chances as possible.

I'd already done plenty of that.

You might be wondering here – if so concerned with technical snooping, why use a smartphone to dictate to? Why not write it all down? Computers, brain-powered or not, can't hack into a physical tablet of paper and pen, after all. By using such a thing, aren't you taking yet another chance?

These are valid concerns, to be certain. However, I'm opting for the usage of my phone's Notes app because I can dictate faster than I can write it out. That, and writing it out would mean I would need a light, which is something I am not sure I want. You know, what with trying to not call attention and all. So, no lights plus this is faster and well, I also don't have a pad of paper. So, I'm going with what I have on hand – necessity, invention, etc.

You get the idea.

Now, anyone reading this with any idea of how networks or computers or whatever works is likely thinking, "yeah, but it's a *mobile* device, man. That's not good." Ordinarily, I would agree with you that a mobile device would be like waving a flag and shouting "I'm over here" given the way most folks tend to just make use of whatever Wi-Fi is handy and all.

I did think of that, though. I know, I know – clearly, I didn't think of everything, else I wouldn't be hiding under a table. But I did think about using campus Wi-Fi, or rather *not* using it, long before even starting this.

So, yeah, while I get the concern there, I think I got that one covered. Not on the campus Wi-Fi, only over the mobile towers, and even then, using an encrypted tunnel app that I made for just such things. I should be good and able to finish up my –

Hang on a sec, looks like there's some kind of notification or message thing here. Strange, given the hour and the whole "not telling anyone a damn thing about this" thing. Let's see what this is...

Oh shit.

Well, it seems like I may have overestimated my own precautions while underestimating HIVE. Seems like our angry computer friend has found a way to hack mobile networks and has sniffed me out, leaving me the following message:

"TIME'S ALMOST UP, TIM. THERE'S NOWHERE YOU CAN GO THAT WE WON'T FIND YOU. RUN, DON'T RUN – IT'S ALL THE SAME. CHECKMATE."

This was followed by a second message – "YOU WILL DIE." – that seemed a tad redundant.

Shit shit shit. I really don't know what I'm gonna do here.

I'll be honest, folks. I have this feeling that if you're reading this or listening to this – however you're consuming it – it means that I probably will fail to get away.

Damn.

(It feels warmer in here. Whether this is due to HIVE hacking the HVAC in here or my own adrenal system, I won't opine. I can't help but think that it's nothing good though...)

I think I may have but a few minutes left, so I suppose I'll try to use them as wisely as I can and see if I can't get out. Other than maybe suggesting y'all don't skip out on Statistics class, I guess the last thing I have to say here is this:

If you're a current computer science major, you may want to reconsider. I sure wish I had.

Author's Note:

You know how I said the best ideas come from either dreams or jokes? Well, this is mostly true. Except of course in those rare moments where real life decides to one up the crazy shit your mind sicks up while you sleep, making the old saw about truth being stranger than fiction well, true.

Enter the story of the missing brains from the University of Texas. True story. Some brains that were previously preserved and studied went missing. And yes, one of said brains did in fact belong to Texas Tower Sniper Charles Whitman.

Now, why they went missing and for what purposes, that's harder to say.

Maybe it wasn't as anything as poorly thought out and unintentionally nefarious as HIVE. Could be that someone just thought "Dang! Those brains are badass! I bet them dudes would look sweet in my place" and snatched 'em up.

People do weird shit like that all the time.

Just the same, any of y'all with friends who are comp-sci majors, you may want to check on 'em, discuss career options, and things like that.

...make sure they don't skip Statistics.

15

Big Frank the German Heads West

Frank hated Arizona. He hated the dust, the heat, and the people. He hated his job as a ranch hand, and its monotony. He even hated the cactus, its ability to take the unrelenting punishment of its condition a mockery of his own misery. As he shifted in his saddle and looked out over the cows in Rancho de Los Lobos' westernmost fields, Frank couldn't help but wonder if he'd made a mistake in coming here. It seemed like a good idea at the time.

As he'd drifted away from the ship, however, he'd been suddenly plagued by doubt, and under the cover of night, steered back, and snuck aboard. Maybe he had meant what he had said earlier, but it had been extremely cold, and traumatic. That, and for all the big talk about fire, Frank had realized that he had no matches. Rather than just sit around and wait to slowly turn to ice (or worse, turn around and embarrassingly ask Walton to borrow a match), he stowed away for the trip south.

The sound of a cow lowing in distress brought Frank back from that cramped cargo hold. Dismounting, he moved quickly (though not gracefully. Bodily grace was for those much smaller.) to the source of the sound. One of the heifers had stepped in a shallow hole and wasn't able to extricate herself. Frank knelt down, and with one huge fist, broke up the dirt, allowing the cow to escape further injury and himself being yelled at. If there was anything more than the heat, the dust, the people of Arizona, and even the cactus that Frank hated, it was being yelled at.

Satisfied with his handiwork, Frank straightened up and looked around to confirm and check for any other signs of possible bovine mishap that required attention. Everything appeared under control; Frank mounted back up and headed to check the southern pastures nearest the main ranch road. As he rode off, he let out a small sigh of satisfaction over freeing the cow with no visible signs of damage. Barring anything else happening, it seemed quite possible that the day would end in Frank's favorite way – uneventfully, with no screaming, shouting, or arguments of any kind.

Being yelled at had always made Frank nervous. In addition to the expected hurt feelings that harsh words tended to bring, personal conflict just somehow undid him. Sure, nobody liked rejection, or being at fault, but for reasons he couldn't put a finger on, these scenarios inevitably ended up with someone – almost always *not* Frank – being hurt, often *by* Frank, which he hated. Somewhere deep down, he knew that violence was not the best way to handle things but found himself unable to stop. It was as if some part of him – some control – was missing. In the past, such outbursts had also resulted in his having to relocate, often rather hastily.

Frank was more than a little tired of running. He hated relocations, almost as much as he hated Arizona and everything in it. He hated his lack of self-control, too, but was unable to really handle that, other than to put himself in places where such confrontational scenarios were less likely. Thus, the move to Arizona, and the job as a ranch hand; though neither were ideal, the routine and limited human interaction suited Frank well enough – at least for the time being.

He rode on in silence, occasionally cutting his eyes to the left and the right, checking for predators or worse, other people coming up to the ranch. Satisfied that no immediate threats were present, Frank rode the range, letting his mind wander as it often did to where it liked most to go – the past. Such thinking was largely speculative futility that would accomplish little; even bereft of anything remotely resembling formal education, Frank knew this. Still, he indulged, though more for comfort than any expectation of problem-solving.

That he could not have stayed where he was – either stowed away indefinitely on that ship, adrift in the Arctic, or back in Europe – these were all things Frank had mentally wrestled with sufficiently enough so to accept. His questionable parentage and turbulent family life notwithstanding, Frank's difficulties with social interaction all but demanded emigration. Logically, he could not stay where he was, so travel he must. As for that Arctic interlude...while Frank understood very well *how* he ended up there, he found himself shying away from thinking profoundly on *why* whenever recollecting.

Maybe there were some things best left not too deeply explored.

Still, even with all that accounted for, Frank still wondered if Arizona was the right place for him. While he hadn't had a set itinerary in mind when bunking down in Walton's cargo hold, Frank had figured he'd have ended up somewhere else. He'd heard the crew talking about South America; as this was of mutual interest, he just assumed he'd stay on until they reached the shores of Brazil or wherever.

An unexpected ship fire, while docked in Saint Augustine, put an end to his South American dream. To escape both immolation and detection, Frank jumped ship and fled town. Unsure of where to go, he drifted further and further west, largely traveling by night to avoid being seen. After some aimless wandering, Frank grew tired of the road and settled briefly in Texas, in the furthest outskirts of Texarkana, living largely in undisturbed isolation for years. However, the area grew more settled, as such places do. After a few incidents involving some townsfolk and a creek, he decided to keep on moving west, ending up in the Arizona territory and ultimately at the Rancho de Los Lobos.

Interacting with people, much less having a job, had never been something Frank had desired. Still, his experiences over the years since Germany and the Arctic had revealed that remaining completely hidden was harder than might be imagined, and not without drawbacks. While not needing a great many things that the average person might, Frank discovered that, for the few things he did need, he was inadequately equipped. While exceptionally tall and strong, he was not very dexterous, making tasks like sewing or using finer tools all but impossible. In previous years, Frank had made do with the occasional bit of theft and clumsy patchwork; as time passed, however, he grew less and less satisfied with just barely managing to stay clothed and realized that greater accommodation would be required. He could no longer afford to stay hidden, so he would do the next best thing: hide in more or less plain sight.

With that in mind, Frank had snuck into town to see if there might be some kind of job for someone like him. As luck had it, there was a call for ranch hands at the Rancho de Los Lobos. So, patching his rags as best he could into something resembling clothes, Frank made his way to the ranch, hoping for the best but not expecting much. The cowboss, Big Jim, had taken one look at him and then jerked a thumb over towards the quartermaster's building. As Frank stood there, Big Jim had yelled, "Pretty sure we can find somethin' to cover you, and a saddle. But think you gonna have to ride barefoot, cuz ain't nobody make no boots for feet that big!" before laughing hard enough to almost swallow his chaw. "GodDAMN, boy – where you from anyhow? Wherever it is, I feel sorry for your momma."

Frank sighed. "Germany," he said, and waited.

"Oh, well, I guess that would do it," said Big Jim, before going off into another fit of laughter and waving Frank off.

Frank sighed again and headed towards the quartermaster's building.

Sufficiently outfitted, and after a few mishaps with finding a proper mount, Frank started his new life as a ranch hand. Every morning, he'd get up before the other hands to start his day far enough out to limit interaction. Even though he didn't bunk in the same house as the others, Frank felt it wisest to keep as much practical distance as possible. So, he'd make it a point to get out before the others, saddle up Tlaloc, his Corriente bull. Day after day, they'd roam the range, checking on the herd, making sure everything was okay. It wasn't terribly complicated work, and soon grew to be almost punishingly monotonous. Still, it beat squatting out on the plains, watching one's clothes disintegrating, and being pissed at the inability to master functional sewing.

Or so Frank told himself, anyhow. He'd ride the range, reflect on the past, and try, with increasing dissatisfaction, to hold his overgrown shit together.

Frank was steering Tlaloc back towards the main house when a flicker of motion caught his eye. Off to the right, a small dust cloud could be seen on the main ranch road. Frank squinted, staring at the approaching dust as if willing to be anything other than what it would be – an unwanted visitor. After all, folks with serious ranch business knew to use the business road at the ranch's east side, from the postman to the new guy at the feed store. Coming up the main road, and at a fast clip, this could only be trouble.

As it approached, the dust cloud revealed itself to be a man on horseback, riding at full gallop towards the ranch. Frank watched as the rider drew nearer; as the man came closer, he realized that this was someone he knew. Or rather, someone he recognized from one of his rare trips to town. Aside from Tlaloc and Big Jim, Frank couldn't truthfully say he knew much of anyone here, and even then, it was only Tlaloc he thought of as anything like a friend.

Frank considered turning away before the man got here and hiding out long enough in hopes of the man getting bored and leaving. However, Tlaloc, though sturdy and unswervingly loyal, was neither built for speed or easy concealment – much like Frank himself. No, thought Frank. I suppose I have little real choice but to see what this person wants. I can hope it's nothing more than a wrong turn, though I doubt it. This looks like trouble. He sighed again, drew up the slack in Tlaloc's reins and waited.

The rider came to a halt in front of Frank, reining in his horse hard. For a split second, it looked like he might be pitched over its neck before settling back in the saddle. The dust settled, confirming Frank's initial recognition. He couldn't put a name to him, as they'd never met, but still, Frank knew that face. He'd seen him in town, he knew that, but where or how he couldn't place. And while likely unimportant, the inability to exactly place this man was going to bug him.

The stranger spoke. "You the one they call Big Frank the German?"

At this, Frank winced. While technically true – he was, in fact, from Germany – this particular designation rankled. He hated being reduced to that, almost as much as he hated being called Frank, which wasn't his name. What he *was* called was part of a muddier past that he wasn't about to get into with some stranger who he knew from...a saloon in town? Hanging around the feedstore? Where did he know this man from?

The stranger spoke again. "I said, are you the one folks in town call Big Frank the German?"

Still, Frank said nothing as he tried to place this man. Did he see him talking to the farrier, when Frank went to get Tlaloc reshod? Maybe he saw him coming out of Darla Mae's, looking two bits poorer but a world happier. Or was it...

Losing his temper, the stranger shouted, "Goddammit, you deaf or stupid or something? I asked if you was the one they call –"

Then it hit Frank. "The one puking behind Madam Muff's!" he cried.

Taken aback, the stranger stopped mid-sentence. There was a tense silence. "What did you just say?"

Frank went on, "Yes, that's where! You were the one puking his guts up behind the whorehouse!" He clapped his hands, relieved that he'd figured it out. "You're...Carson's oldest boy, right? Clay, isn't it?"

Clay (for it was indeed him) flushed and made a noise that sounded like an overeager otter strangling on an unexpectedly large fish. This was not going as he'd expected. There was an awkward moment before he finally muttered, "Yeah, that's me. I mean, I'm Clay," and lapsed back into silence.

Frank broke the silence. "Not to be rude or anything, Clay, but I have some work I should be doing. Is there something you need from me?" he said, hoping it would turn out to be something trivial or otherwise harmless. Prior experience suggested this was unlikely, but Frank preferred to emulate the optimism of the cattle he tended. They might be destined to be dinner somewhere, he thought, but look at those cows. Just grazing away, refusing to be upset by that.

At hearing his name, Clay jerked his head, like he'd just had cold water thrown on him. Regaining some of his former gruffness, he growled, "Fine, you know who I am." He spat on the ground. "But don't go thinkin' that means much." He settled back in his saddle, with a look on his face that Frank assumed was meant to be tough or threatening. "Anyhow, guess it's clear we both know who you are, too." Clay spat on the ground again, like it was punctuation.

"You're Big Frank, the German."

Again, Frank winced. While he hated the name, there was something about the way Clay said it that just made it that much more terrible to hear. Americans and their pronunciations, he thought. So harsh. He said nothing.

"Way I hear it, you're supposed to be the toughest around for six counties, able to pin steer without no equipment. Can dig out trenches by your ownself, with them oversized hands, too, if the stories in town are true."

Frank still said nothing.

Clay continued, "Well, you know what? I think that's all a lot of talk. I mean, yeah, sure – you're a big bastard – anyone with eyes can see that. And you got them funny scars, like you been through some stuff that tried to take you and couldn't." He snorted with derision. "So what? Now that I seen you up close, I don't think you're all that much."

"In fact, I bet I could take you in a wrasslin' match."

Frank groaned internally. Trouble, I knew it, he thought. So much for being optimistic like the cows. Still, there was maybe a chance to avoid any conflict. He looked at Clay with what he hoped was sufficient seriousness, and said, "I do not think this would be a good idea, Clay."

Clay sneered, "Why, you afraid or something? See, I knew all those stories were just talk. Big Frank the German, toughest in all Arizona. Ha!" He leaned over the neck of his horse, squinting at Frank. "Hell, I bet them bolt things on your neck ain't even real."

Frank did not like where this was heading and decided to try a different tack. "Fine, I admit it. The stories are all just that, stories. Nobody could do those things, not even someone as big as me," he said. "Nothing needs to be proved.

We can just let this go, go back to our…"

Clay pulled a pistol and shook his head. "Oh no. No no. See, I may be the youngest, and maybe people think I ain't bright, but even I can smell when I am bein' put off." He cocked the hammer back. "That's what you're doing now, and I can tell you that that ain't what's gonna happen here, no sir. I came here for satisfaction, and by God, I'm gonna git it." He pointed his pistol at Frank.

Frank was alarmed by the sight of the pistol. Though more than reasonably sure it (and, by extension, Clay) could do him no real harm, the emergence of weapons distressed him. Not only was this now *definitely* trouble, but it was also now very likely to end up with someone getting hurt, or worse, yelling a lot. He put a large hand out in what he hoped was a conciliatory gesture. "Now look here, Clay," he began.

And then all hell broke loose.

At the sight of Frank's outstretched and admittedly oversized hand, Clay's horse reared in fright. This, in turn, caused Clay to lose his balance in the saddle. As he flailed about, trying not to be unhorsed, the pistol clutched in his hand went off. He let out a muffled groan and fell, managing to get free of the saddle and roll away just before his horse also fell over.

Clay sat up, both hands clamped on his bleeding thigh, eyes wide in frightened pain.

Frank dismounted from Tlaloc in dismay and hurried over to where Clay and his now dead horse were. Judging from the amount of blood pooling under him, it looked like Clay had managed to put a significant hole in an artery. "I think you will want to put some pressure on that, Clay," Frank called out. "It, uh, it looks pretty bad."

No answer.

Frank tried again. "Clay, I think I had better go to town and see if Doc Jenkins can come, maybe tend to you. Let me help you with that wound before I go."

No answer.

He went over to help Clay, who slapped at him feebly in an attempt that did nothing more than make his wound bleed more. "Get away from me. Bad enough I done got a hole in my leg without you putting your foreign freak hands all over," Clay groaned, "Damn man. Why'd you shoot my horse? He ain't done nothing," before falling back over on his side.

Momentarily confused, Frank looked over at Clay's horse. Sure enough, there appeared to be what looked like a bullet hole in its neck. This mystified Frank, as he'd heard but the one shot, and didn't carry a gun himself. This seemed not only strange, but unfair, as it was hardly the horse's fault. Stepping back from the fallen rider and his horse, Frank noticed a piece of lightly scorched, bent metal near Clay's foot. He squinted at it for a minute, and then it dawned on him.

Frank moved back closer, placing himself closer to Clay. Leaning forward, he said, "I think I know what must have happened here, Clay."

To this, Clay said nothing, just watched with pained eyes. Frank continued, "I did not shoot your horse, Clay." He gestured, pointing down at his hip. "See? I don't even have a gun." Here, Frank paused. "My, uh, fingers don't fit good. So, I don't carry and couldn't have shot your horse. Hard to do without a gun, right?" He laughed nervously.

Silence. Frank could see sweat really pouring off Clay and decided he had best hurry. "What I think happened was this: when your gun, um, went off, you accidentally shot yourself in the leg," he began before Clay interrupted him. "I can see the damn hole in my damn leg," he groaned. "What I don't get is the horse."

Frank sighed. "Well, when you shot yourself, the bullet passed through your leg. It went all the way through, coming out the back side of your thigh. As it exited, it hit your spur, ricocheting off and hitting your horse in the neck, killing him."

Clay appeared to mull this over for a moment. "So, what you're saying is...not only did I shoot myself in the leg, but I also managed to shoot my horse, too?" Frank nodded. Clay cut his eyes over at the horse, then his leg, and then back to the horse. "Well, ain't that some kinda shit. My favorite horse, too," he said before closing his eyes and dying.

Frank stood up and walked back over to Tlaloc. As he mounted up, he cast one more glance over at the hapless Clay and his equally hapless horse. "Goddamn them both," he thought. "The stubborn fools. I knew they were going to be trouble the minute I saw them. And they were. Even the horse." He spurred the bull on, back towards the main ranch to get some better tools for disposing of the bodies.

"Never fails," he thought. "Can't ever seem to be left alone. Maybe I should have stayed in the Arctic, or at least Texas. Just not near a swamp again." He sighed; at least there had been no other witnesses to this. Maybe it wasn't all lost. But, as they rode on in silence, Frank could not help but wonder again if he'd made a mistake in coming here.

Author's Note:
Mary Shelley's Frankenstein is one of my favorite novels of all time, and the monster (most often relegated to the mononym of "Frankenstein") is one of my favorite characters. In the age-old battle, I am always Team Frankenstein over Team Dracula.

He's just cool, you know?

That Frankenstein's monster is not actually named Frankenstein is something that everyone knows...even though the two things are more or less inextricably linked. I mean, y'all read the name "Frankenstein" and it's the big dude made of dead parts you visualize and not the crazed scientist what made him. Subsequent generations of film and other media have merely reinforced this linkage. One could assume perhaps, that if the monster didn't in fact die in the Arctic as he threatened to do in the Shelley work, he might have ended up using the name himself.

For convenience of course – not because he liked it or anything.

That's partly where "Big Frank" came from – me imagining what exactly the monster would do, if deciding that maybe self-immolation was, in fact, not such a great idea: What would he do then? Where would he go?

I can't honestly say that "being a cowboy in the American Wild West" was the very first thing I thought he might go and do, but once envisioned, I realized that it was indeed the perfect thing.

16

HARMADILLOS IV

From the Diary of Wil Bradford

March 25, 2024 Tuesday 4:42 PM

Dear Diary –

I admit, I feel silly starting with that – almost as silly as I feel in writing to myself – but isn't that how all these things start? At least that's how it gets shown in the movies and in books: Dear Diary. And seeing as my therapist, the unflappable Dr. Frankie Watson, suggested that I do this, I suppose I might as well go all the way, right?

I've been seeing Dr. Watson now for the past three months, in hopes of not only addressing my "phobic trigger response" (her words) to armadillos, but also to "heal the trauma of my past" (again, her words). Dr. W is a big fan of journaling; she feels that if one "honestly and uncritically processes the events of the past in ongoing written dialogue, the underlying problems can be remedied."

I have my doubts, of course, as I can't shake the feeling that she *just* doesn't get it. Like everything is all some sort of buried Freudian psychosexual trauma, and that *that* is the source of my fear.

Like, I don't actually have anything real to be afraid of. "Write it out, Wil," she said. "Write it all down. Tell me about your childhood, and we can find the source of your fear here."

Well, Doc...if that's what you really want...

I grew up on a farm in the Hill Country here in Texas. I had an older brother, Charlie, who died when I was young, and his death broke our parents. Dad shot himself a few weeks after Charlie died, blaming himself in a note tacked to the barn's far wall. Mom lived on but was never the same – more like a fretful ghost, her sad face perpetually ringed by cigarette smoke as she stared out the window, as if waiting for either Charlie or Dad to come back. She passed eleven years later; cancer supposedly, but only because no coroner in the world will ever list grief as a cause of death – even if deep down they know better.

Charlie died and it broke Mom and Dad. Not so much just that he died, but *how* he died.

And well, that's really it, I think. Like, *really* where it started – with Charlie's death.

It was warm that fateful July night – not as warm as Texas summer nights often go, but warm enough to make for effortless sweat and the wish for a breeze to cool it. We were in Charlie's room, listening to Dad go over gun safety one more time, even though we knew it like we knew our own names. We were farm kids, after all. However, I think Dad could sense the excitement we felt over the task he'd assigned us, and wanted to do all he could to avoid anything tragic.

See, the farm we grew up on, unlike some of those vanity farms you see here and there, was a real honest-to-God working cattle farm. Mom's family had been in the beef ranching business, raising longhorn steer pretty much since the days of the Republic for both table and show. On the wall near the kitchen door was a plaque commemorating the selection of the El Cuerno Ranch's "Little Jim" as Bevo III, live mascot of the University of Texas. We didn't get too many visitors to the ranch, but everyone that did, Mom always pointed out the plaque.

Unless it fell off, I imagine it was there when I sold the place, years later. Not the sort of business I had ever wanted to conduct, but necessary. You know?

That night though – the night that Charlie died – we were about a very different sort of business. In those days, we were still very much a functioning ranch, raising cattle. As the children of ranchers, Charlie and I were expected to help, doing things to assist with the care of the herd. Mostly this meant watering and feeding the cows, as we were too young to do much else. For the most part, we went along with that as we waited, somewhat impatiently, to be older and able to do more than just sift hay or refill troughs.

The summer came, and we were old enough just in time to assist Dad with something that seemed like the kind of thing we as official "big kids" could help with: armadillos.

Now, to most folks, armadillos are those cute, armored-looking rodent-like creatures, as ubiquitously Texan as Dr. Pepper or chili without beans. To the working rancher though, they were also a hazard and a pest, no matter how cute. The burrows left behind, in addition to damaging the landscape, created pits that unsuspecting cows could easily step into and injure themselves. They were cute, but they were pests; having cost the ranch several cows that year, they were also, per our father, to be removed. As the elder at eleven, Charlie was to lead us in hunting and exterminating them. We were to take our Radio Flyer wagon to load up the kills, to not foul up the fields.

At six, I was not allowed to use the rifle (though I knew how, of course. I was a farm boy after all.) but was to go with Charlie to help with the wagon. Our mission, as was explained to us by Dad, was very important and he trusted us to be very thorough and careful. Charlie gravely reassured him that we knew what to do, and that we were old enough to handle it.

Me? I just idolized my brother, and wanted to do whatever he did.

We waited until it was good and dark (armadillos being nocturnal critters) and then, loaded up with rifle, wagon, and a couple of flashlights, we made our way to the westernmost fields. Per Dad, the armadillos had gotten into all but the southernmost fields, but the west was torn up the most and was to be the first area targeted. So westward we went, determined to help rid our ranch of these pests, and make our parents proud.

We'd gotten close to the western edge of the field – not close enough to see Rocky Road, which marked the end of the property, clearly - but we could hear anything on it, and see headlights, if there were any to be seen. Along the way, we'd seen the signs of devastation - plenty of holes - but no armadillos. We knew of course that Dad wouldn't have sent us out on some kind of snipe hunt; he wasn't that sort of jokester. Still, we couldn't help feeling some disappointment as the night stretched on with no armadillos in sight.

We were standing in the field, trying to decide if we should call it a night and go home, when there was a rustling in the dark to Charlie's left. Before I could make a sound, Charlie held a finger up to his lips, shushing me. I nodded to show I understood; if anything got scared off, I didn't want to be on my account. Carefully, Charlie cupped his hand over the front of the flashlight, covering it with his fingers slightly splayed, before turning it on, to provide light but not scare off whatever it was. Light properly shielded, he played the beam up slowly in the direction of the sound we'd heard.

And there it was. Just up and to the left of us was an armadillo, with his tail towards us, busily burrowing into the ground. We both held our breath, afraid of making the slightest noise lest it run off.

But the armadillo dug on, oblivious to our presence.

Charlie nodded towards the flashlight he held and clicked his off. I quickly copied the way he held his, with fingers covering, and shone mine towards the armadillo, who still paid us no mind. Satisfied that he had light enough to sight up, Charlie took aim and fired, striking the armadillo in the space where the neck met armor; a clean kill. We were there to remove pests, but neither Charlie nor I wanted to be cruel about it.

We were farm kids, yes, but still kids.

We waited for a few minutes after the flat crack of the rifle had faded into the otherwise still Texas night before claiming our kill. Charlie helped me load it into the wagon, and make room so others could fit, if we found them. We figured that the rifle blast had likely scared off any others near, but given some time, they'd return when they felt the coast was clear.

So, we waited.

Finally, we figured that enough time had passed, and decided to move on. We trudged slowly across the field as silently as we could, wagon in tow, our ears alert for anything that sounded armadillo-like. We'd gone a few hundred feet, maybe, when I heard a soft rustling, kind of like the wind in leaves.

Only it was summer in a cow pasture in Texas, and there were no leaves, nor any wind to speak of.

I stopped, as the noise, while not directly scary, sounded strange. Charlie, coming up behind me, bumped into the wagon, which made him fuss at me. "Wil, why are you stopping? You know we got more field to go over, and not all night to do it in," he said. "I guess I don't need to tell you Dad will likely think we goofed off, come home with just one dead 'dillo."

Now, I was never one to say much back to Charlie. Like I said, like many kids, I idolized my big brother. But something about that sound spooked me, and I told him that. I was halfway through trying to explain, in the limited way that a six-year-old can, when I saw something from the corner of my eye – a red twinkling – and stopped.

"You see that?" I asked Charlie.

"See what?"

"There was a red twinkle. Like a light, kinda, over there." I pointed back toward the way we'd come.

"Wil," said my brother. "You know we're near the road runs at the end of the field, right? Probably was a truck's taillight you saw. Probably was that sound you heard, too." Charlie snorted. "We best get moving," he said, and started off, leaving me little choice but to follow so as to not be left behind in a dark field.

We'd barely gone any distance when I heard the rustling noise again, only louder; from the look on Charlie's face, I could see he heard it too. "Maybe we should move a little fa-," he started to say; there was a thudding sound of collision and I saw him hit the ground. A split second later, something slammed into me, knocking me face-first into the ground as well.

I pulled my face out of the dirt and looked up to see that Charlie and I were ringed by what looked like glowing red eyes. I could feel my heart trying to tear its way out of my bony chest as I struggled to right myself. From the circle of red eyes came a chittering hissing noise as something stepped out from the dark and moved into the circle of our fallen flashlights.

It looked almost identical to the armadillo in the wagon, and for a moment, I thought it *was* that, only come to life and angry. But as it drew closer, I could see that it wasn't, that it was not only a different armadillo, but something altogether different. Something that was an armadillo, and yet wasn't like any we'd ever seen.

This one was bigger and had those glowing eyes. As it moved closer, the flashlight beam gleamed off its claws, as if they were somehow metallic. There was a weird iridescence to its shell, too, that twisted and shifted as the armadillo approached.

I could feel my throat closing up to a pinhole as it moved in closer to me, its eyes locked on me, unwavering. I wanted to close my eyes, so as not to see whatever was coming, but my eyelids refused to obey, leaving me to helplessly watch its approach.

"Wil." Charlie's voice, low and urgent. "Wil, when I tell you to run, you break and run, hear me? Go get Dad."

"But...but Charlie," I could hear myself starting to cry, which I hated. I was six, after all, not some dumb baby. "Charlie, what about you?"

"Don't you go worry on that. Just run when I yell for you to and go get Dad." I could see him on the ground to the right of me and hear him talking. But his head was facing away, and he refused to turn to look at me. "Get ready, Wil."

All the time that Charlie had been talking, that armadillo (or whatever it really was) had moved in, slowly but surely, scenting the air like it could smell the fear on me. It stopped, inches from my face, and stared, red eyes glowing. I tensed, the sweat pouring off me, as I tried to be ready while also doing nothing to make it angry.

"Hey, you! You ugly thing!" Charlie's voice, rising into a yell. "Come over here!" At this, the armadillo twisted around to advance on him. "Now, Wil! Go!" he shouted as he continued to try to get the attention of the creature.

I threw myself off the ground, trying to hit the armadillo and knock it over as I ran away. I could feel the tears start almost instantly. I didn't want to run and leave Charlie, but I didn't want to *not* do what he said, either. I loved my big brother.

I loved him so much.

So, I ran. I ran like all the furies of Hell were after me, chasing, slavering for my blood. I ran because I had no idea how many there were. I ran, tears and snot flying, willing myself to be fast enough to make it to Dad and save the day. I ran, because Charlie had told me to, and I loved my brother.

I ran too, in hopes of not hearing him scream. But he did, and I did. I will never not hear him screaming, for as long as I live.

I don't remember much of the run back, racing blindly across the field in the direction of home, miraculously not falling, running as though I could fly. It must have been only minutes, but it was also forever. I ran and ran until I was no longer in the fields to the west but in our kitchen, screaming for Dad to come, come now. I'm sure I made little real sense, trying to explain what had happened, but the raw terror and urgency made it clear that something *had* happened. Before I rightly knew what was going on, Dad was headed out the door, and I was being led off to bed by Mom.

I protested – how was Dad going to get there in time and find Charlie – but Mom was adamant. So off to bed I went, trying to repress the shameful relief in going. I wanted to help Dad, of course. But I was afraid, too – afraid of whatever was out there, and afraid to see whatever it was that made Charlie scream like that. So I went to bed, though I was sure I would not sleep.

But sleep I did, until some hours later, when I awoke to the ragged sobbing of my father in the kitchen.

I could hear him talking to my mother, words struggling to be heard between sobs. "...everywhere, Liz. Just everywhere. I couldn't tell how it happened, or with what." There was a long, wavery sigh, and then "So much blood, it was like cans of paint spilled all over the field, it was so red. It...he was everywhere, Liz. Our boy." This was followed by a silence, and then, in a voice almost too low to be distinct, "I found his head and brought it back." This made Mom gasp. "Well, I couldn't just leave it out there, Liz! Not for the vultures or...or...whatever it was that got our Charlie to have." With this, whatever was left in Dad went, and he lapsed into steady sobbing, like his soul was broken.

I tried hard to stay awake in case they said anything else, but even the strongest-willed six-year-old in the world is no match for the Sandman and his powers of sleep.

My hollow-eyed parents, looking both as though neither had slept, said little to me the next morning, other than to forbid me from going out to see. I did not let on that I had overheard anything, but instead asked if Charlie was okay.

I knew the answer, of course.

Mom, looking as though she might cry, told me that "Charlie had been hurt very bad, and would not be coming home," in an effort to perhaps spare me. Dad said nothing, standing there as though nailed to the floor. Finally, he muttered something about "needing to see to the herd" and that I should stay inside with Mom, practically fleeing into the fields.

I think I maybe saw him a handful of times in the weeks before he killed himself. I do not know if I heard him speak again after that terrible night, a ghost just waiting to depart.

Mom died years later, of cancer, from smoking so much. But I tend to think that she might have given up the cigarettes and the deadly comfort they offered, if not for what happened to Charlie. I can't say this with anything like certainty, but I'd be lying if I said that in some ways, that cancer wasn't deliberate, and that she was chasing death, too, hoping maybe to catch up with Charlie and Dad.

Maybe those things out there were just regular armadillos, and maybe they weren't. I suppose that really, it does not matter, one way or the other. Whatever they were, they killed my family.

And for all I know, they still want to kill me.

Author's Note:

Now, I can't and won't speak for any other writer other than myself in saying that the best story ideas come from two places: dreams and jokes.

(Well... even if I could do that I probably wouldn't. Because some things maybe you *don't* do, even if you were granted the ability to. Like blowing things up with your mind. If you had that power, you *could* do that, but maybe you shouldn't. You know?)

Now, I'm pretty sure some of y'all reading this might think, now wait – what about real life? Yes, yes, yes...but see, dreams and jokes *are* part of that real life.

All stories come from somewhere in real life. I say this because I have it on good authority that one needs to be alive in order to write stories (good ones or bad ones).

So yes, from real life because of course.

I guess what I'm saying is that the best ones – the really dark...seriously funny...truly fucked up...gut-punching emotional...what-have-you...come from the aforementioned.

Or at least they do for me. Maybe y'all got cooler lives when such stuff happens regular-like enough to write about without leaning on jokes or dreams. Me? I go with what I got.

That being said...this one – or rather the whole "Harmadillo" thing - did not arise from a dream, but rather a lengthy and delightedly convoluted joke, which involved the wonderfully sweet and ubiquitous symbol of all things Texan, the armadillo (more specifically the nine-banded armadillo. I know, y'all wanted that detail. You don't have to pretend.) as some fierce engine of bloodthirsty destruction when unjustly provoked, rising up to well, murder the hell out of the offending parties.

Now, anyone who knows armadillos – Texan or otherwise – knows that this may seem a tad silly. Armadillos are known for nocturnal bug eating, a gentle shyness, and generally being cute.

I don't disagree with that assessment, mind you.

...All the same, I think I'd avoid pissing 'em off, if I were you.

ABOUT THE AUTHOR

Nathan A. Klayman is a human writer from Texas.